"Cards on the table, Matt?"

He wasn't going to be dealt a good hand but he nodded anyway.

"Your being back in Boston on a short-term basis doesn't work for me."

"Care to explain that?"

"You and I worked because we met up, had a great time and went our separate ways. You were a burst of sunshine in my life, an escape, a fantasy." DJ pulled her bottom lip between her teeth and forced herself to meet his eyes. "That's not who I am here, in Boston."

"Who are you in Boston?"

"Controlled. Driven. Exceptionally busy. What we had worked for so long because when I was with you, I was with you one hundred percent. So if you think that because you are going to be in Boston for the foreseeable future that we are going to roll back into bed, that's not going to happen."

Fantasy or not, surface or not, convenient or not...

They were headed for bed.

Their chemistry was too combustible for that not to happen.

* * *

Hot Christmas Kisses is part of the Love in Boston series from Joss Wood!

Dear Reader,

Christmas in the Southern Hemisphere is superhot, and I so enjoyed writing a book where I could, virtually, experience a snowy Christmas!

DJ Winston is a partner in Winston and Brogan, a fast-rising design house situated in Boston, Massachusetts. DJ deals with the business end; she finds numbers so much easier to deal with than people. After growing up with her dysfunctional parents, she is not interested in opening herself up to love, but she has had, for many years, what she thinks is the perfect relationship...

For the past seven years, Matt Edwards, a well-respected human rights lawyer, has had a no-commitments, on-off, when-it-suits affair with Dylan-Jane, and it's worked well. They both know the score: some fun times, in bed and out, a few laughs and no expectations or drama.

But when Matt returns to Boston to deal with his past, he and DJ—unable to jump on a plane and run back to their own lives—have to learn to deal with each other, and finally realize that the life they want is the one they create together.

Happy reading,

Joss

Connect with me at www.josswoodbooks.com.

Twitter: @josswoodbooks

Facebook: Joss Wood Author

JOSS WOOD

HOT CHRISTMAS KISSES

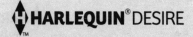

Recycling programs
for this product may
not exist in your area.

ISBN-13: 978-1-335-97180-7

Hot Christmas Kisses

Copyright © 2018 by Joss Wood

Printed in U.S.A.

Joss Wood loves books and traveling—especially to the wild places of Southern Africa and, well, anywhere. She's a wife, a mom to two teenagers and slave to two cats. After a career in local economic development, she now writes full-time. Joss is a member of Romance Writers of America and Romance Writers of South Africa.

Books by Joss Wood

Harlequin Desire

Convenient Cinderella Bride
The Nanny Proposal

The Ballantyne Billionaires

His Ex's Well-Kept Secret
One Night to Forever
The CEO's Nanny Affair
Little Secrets: Unexpectedly Pregnant

Love in Boston

Friendship on Fire
Hot Christmas Kisses

Visit her Author Profile page at Harlequin.com, or josswoodbooks.com, for more titles.

Prologue

Christmas, the year before

In a rural part of Devon, three thousand miles from her home in Boston, Massachusetts, DJ Winston smoothed her hands over the maroon-and-silver dress and turned to face her computer screen.

Her two best friends, twins Darby and Jules Brogan, lounged on Jules's couch in her office back in Massachusetts, coffee cups on the table in front of them. As was their custom, they'd shortly be closing their business for the Christmas break, ending the year by treating their staff to lunch.

"Send everybody my love and tell them I hope they have a lovely minivacation."

DJ ignored Darby rolling her eyes at DJ's inability to wish anyone a merry Christmas. She tried, she really did, but the words always got stuck in her throat. *Merry Christmas! Happy holidays! Ho, ho, ho*…nope, she couldn't do it. She could talk interest rates and contract terms, equity and cash flow, but she stuttered and stammered her way through December. The festive—hah!—season made her feel like she was eight again, alone, frightened and wondering why neither of her parents loved her.

DJ knew the twins would like to discuss her antipathy toward Christmas, but it was, like so many other subjects, off-limits.

DJ adored the twins, but she believed in keeping some distance between her and the people she loved. Distance was her safety net, her belay rope, her life vest. Distance was how she'd always protected herself. And since it had worked for her as a child and as a teen, what was the point of changing her strategy now?

Darby cocked her head to one side. "That dress looks fantastic with your dark hair and eyes, DJ."

Jules nodded her agreement. "Vibrant colors suit you. But with your height and build, anything looks good on you, you know that."

She didn't, though.

While the twins saw her as attractive, she still saw herself as the gangly, dark-haired teenager who embarrassed her blond, blue-eyed mother. DJ was smart enough, Fenella reluctantly admitted, but she was too tall, too lanky, with not enough charm. So Fenella said when she was in a good mood.

DJ tried not to remember the words Fenella let fly when she was angry.

"What shoes are you wearing?" Darby asked.

"My Jimmy Choos, the ones you made me buy last week." DJ nodded to the sexy silver shoes on the bed.

"So…" Darby drawled. "When is Matt arriving?"

DJ released an irritated sigh. "He's not."

"He stood you up? Nice Christmas present." Jules was sarcasm personified.

DJ sighed. Darby and Jules didn't understand that her and Matt Edwards's ad hoc arrangement worked for them, as it had for the past six years. Depending on their schedules, she and Matt met for a night or a weekend. That was when DJ stepped out of her life, pushing aside numbers and profit margins, cash-flow issues and cost projections. When she was with Matt, she allowed herself the freedom to be another version of herself—fun-loving, exuberant and sensuous.

Neither she nor Matt had any expectations, and DJ was very conscious of the fact that, despite making this unusual situation last for many years, their arrangement was a temporary thing.

They had no ties to each other, nothing to bind them except for the expectation of good sex, a few laughs and a relaxing time spent in undemanding company. She didn't need more. A partner, boyfriend or permanent lover wasn't something she wanted for herself; after being abandoned by her father and rejected by Fenella, DJ wasn't prepared to hand over her battered heart to another human to kick around. She was keeping possession of that fragile organ.

Spontaneous weekends spent with Matt worked well for her, but yesterday he'd blown her off, saying that he, despite it being Christmas, needed to stay in the Netherlands, to consult with a client who was in a world of hurt. Because Matt was a fantastically successful human-rights lawyer, *hurt* could mean his client was a political refugee ducking prison time, or a tribe of aboriginal people who'd been kicked off their ancestral land and were facing the imminent loss of their culture and way of life.

The fact that his on-and-off lover needed to escape Christmas and was horny as hell didn't nudge the needle of his what-international-laws-did-this-violate? scale.

DJ had considered missing her friend's wedding but that meant *doing* Christmas in Boston. Ugh. Attending this Christmas Eve wedding was the lesser of two evils.

Her friends on the screen were still waiting for her response. Right, they'd been discussing Matt's nonarrival. "We have an understanding that work always comes first. He's tied up doing something terribly important."

What he wasn't doing was her.

DJ pulled a face, glanced at the corner clock on her laptop screen and sighed. "I'd better slap on some makeup or else I'm going to be late for the church service."

Darby frowned and waved at DJ's dress. "Take that off first. You do not want to get makeup on that dress."

Good point. Friends since kindergarten, she was superbly comfortable disrobing in front of them. Allowing them to see her messed-up inner world was what she found difficult. DJ gently pulled the dress over her head and laid it on the bed.

Jules whistled. "Push-up bra, tiny thong, heels. Edwards has no idea what he's missing out on."

"I agree."

That voice.

DJ whipped her head up and looked toward the doorway. Her heart, stupid thing, did cartwheels in her chest.

Matt, a shoulder pressed to the doorframe, looked as effortlessly sexy as he always did. A tall blond with deep green eyes and a surfer's tan, he had the face and body to advertise sun, sea and sex. He didn't look like what he was: a brilliant international lawyer with a steel-trap mind.

The moisture in DJ's mouth disappeared and it took all her willpower not to run to him and start removing his clothes. She desperately wanted to slide the cream linen jacket down his arms and rip apart his navy button-down shirt. The leather belt would be next, and she'd soon have the buttons of his designer jeans undone. In her hand he'd be hot and hard...

It had always been this way. Matt just had to look at her with those incredibly green eyes and she went from cool and collected to crazy in ten seconds flat. She didn't love him—hell, she barely knew him—but, damn, she craved his mouth, his hands on all her long neglected and secret places.

Okay, try to hold it together. For God's sake, be cool.

"I thought you couldn't make it," DJ said, wincing at the happy note in her voice. *Yeah, opposite of cool, Winston.*

She glanced at her dress lying on the bed, considered slipping it on and then shrugged. Why bother? Matt had seen everything she had, more than once.

Matt stepped into the room, walking with a grace not many big men possessed. "My client was delayed."

Matt crossed the room to her and his hand lifted to cradle her face, his thumb brushing across her lower lip. He looked down, and she felt the heat of his gaze on the tiny triangle low on her hips and her equally frivolous bra. She was, in turn, both entranced and brutally turned on by the passion flaring in his eyes. Being wanted by this sexy man always shot a ray of enhanced sunshine through her veins.

"Nice outfit, Dylan-Jane," Matt said when their eyes locked again, his voice extra growly.

He was the only person, apart from her mother,

who'd ever called her by her full name, and on Matt's lips it was a caress rather than a curse.

"Hi."

The single-syllable greeting was all her tangled tongue could manage.

"Hi back." Matt lowered his mouth to hers and as their lips touched they both hesitated, as they always did. DJ had no idea why Matt waited but she enjoyed stretching out the moment, ramping up the anticipation. Yes, she was desperate for his touch, but she also wanted to make the moment last. The first kiss, after so long apart, was always exceptional.

Finally, Matt's clever mouth touched hers and it was, as always, sweet and sexy—a little rediscovery and a whole bunch of familiarity. The kisses they'd exchange later would be out of control, like a wildfire, but this one was tender and, in its way, as souldeep sexy as what would come later.

Talking about later...

It took everything DJ had to pull her mouth off his, to drop her hands from that wide, warm chest. "If we don't get dressed we're going to be late for the wedding."

"Yeah, you have about fifteen minutes to get out of that room to beat the bride to the church."

DJ yelped at Darby's dry voice. DJ took a step to the side to look past Matt's arm to the computer screen. Her friends were still there, both looking worried. DJ was thankful that they'd only had a view of Matt's broad back and truly excellent butt during that kiss.

"Hey, Matt," Darby said.

Matt pinched the bridge of his nose, shook his head and rolled his eyes at DJ. With a rueful smile he turned around and looked at the screen. "Ladies."

"Well done for arriving in the nick of time," Jules said, her voice tart.

Matt just raised one sandy, arrogant eyebrow. Then he stepped up to the desk, looked down at the screen and smiled. "'Bye, ladies." He closed the lid to the laptop and turned back to face DJ.

"I've missed you."

DJ tipped back her head to look into his eyes, her cynical side wondering if he said that as a way to talk her into bed. But the look on his face was sincere, his eyes radiating honesty. Besides, Matt didn't use coercion. She was either fully on board or he backed off; Matt did not whine or beg or force.

Besides, they both knew she was going to slide into bed with him the moment she saw him standing in the doorway. She was putty in his hands.

"You, half-naked in sexy lingerie, is my early Christmas present." Matt lifted a curl off her forehead and tucked it behind her ear. His mouth curled up into a deprecating half smile. "But I'm embarrassed to tell you that I hightailed it out of my office to make my flight and I've been rushing ever since. I didn't want to be late, so I didn't stop to buy condoms. You wouldn't happen to have any, would you?"

DJ shook her head. Well, crap. Matt never, ever made love to her without one.

"So, damn. No condoms. Maybe we should go to the church and pick this up later."

Oh, hell, no.

"Or we could just carry on…" DJ ran her finger down his hard erection before fumbling with the snap on his pants.

Matt groaned. "Dylan-Jane, oral isn't enough. I need to be inside you. I'll go pick up some condoms and come back. We'll miss the service, but we could still make the reception."

Hearing his rough, growly, frustrated voice, DJ melted. "I'm on the pill, Matt. I'm clean, there hasn't been anyone since we last hooked up, and if you can tell me you are…"

Matt nodded. "Yeah, I am." He kissed her lips before pulling back again. "Can I trust you with this, Dylan-Jane? There won't be any unexpected surprises?"

If he knew her better, he wouldn't have to ask. Sure, the time they spent together was a fantasy, hot and wild, but that wasn't the person she was in real life. In Boston, she didn't do the unexpected and she hated surprises. Her life was planned, regulated, controlled.

And a baby was Darby's dream, not DJ's.

"I've got this, Matt." DJ pushed his pants and boxers down his hips, wound her arms around his strong neck and lowered her mouth onto his, whispering her words against his lips. "Come inside me, Matt, it's been too damn long."

Matt didn't hesitate, quickly pushing her panties to the side. He slid inside her, held her there and then lowered her to the bed. Gathering her to him, DJ knew that he'd try to be a gentleman—he always tried to make their first encounter together slow and reverential. She didn't need either—she needed hot and hard and fast.

"Matt, I need to burn," DJ told him in a tortured whisper.

Matt pushed himself up and slowly rolled his hips. When she released a low moan, he smiled.

He had a repertoire of smiles, from distracted to dozy, but this one was her favorite: part pirate, part choirboy, all wicked.

"Well, then, let's light a match, Dylan-Jane."

Matt slid his hands under her hips, lifted her up, slammed into her and catapulted her into that white-hot, delicious fire she'd longed for.

She was almost, but not quite, tempted to murmur "Merry Christmas to me."

One

Nearly a year later...

In the public area at Logan International Airport, Matt Edwards ignored the crowds and maneuvered his way around the flower bearers and card holders. He'd mastered the art of walking and working his smartphone: there were ten messages from his office and a few text messages. None, dammit, were from Dylan-Jane.

Despite reaching out over a week ago, she'd yet to give him a definitive answer about them getting together in Boston.

Maybe she was making him wait because he'd been out of touch for so long. But he'd been busy and it just happened that they'd had less contact this year than usual. A lot less. But he was here now, and he was hopeful they could recapture some of their old magic.

"Matt!"

Matt turned, saw the tall frame of his old friend Noah Lockwood striding toward him and smiled. Well, this was a pleasant surprise.

Matt pushed his phone into the inside pocket of his black jacket before shaking Noah's hand. "It's great to see you, but what are you doing here?"

Noah fell into step beside him. "I've just dropped Jules off. She's flying to New York to meet a client. I knew you were coming in today, saw the flight times and thought I'd buy you a beer."

An excellent plan. It had been months, maybe even more than a year, since he and Noah had exchanged anything other than a brief phone call or a catch-up email. At college, they'd been tight, and despite their busy lives, he still considered Noah a friend.

Noah had also introduced Matt to DJ, and for that he'd always be grateful.

"I'd love a beer."

They walked to the nearest bar and Matt headed to two empty seats at the far end of the joint, tucking his suitcase between him and the wall before he slid onto the barstool. Within minutes he had a glass of an expensive microbrew in front of him.

Noah raised his glass and an enquiring eyebrow. "What brings you back to Boston?"

How to answer? Matt ignored the ache in that triangle where his ribs met. This visit, unlike those quick visits to see his grandfather, was going to be… difficult.

Emotional. Draining. Challenging.

All the things he most tried to avoid.

"I'm moving my grandfather into an assisted-living facility." Stock answer.

Noah looked surprised. "The judge is moving out of his home? Why?"

Matt took a sip of his beer before rubbing his eyes. "He's showing signs of dementia and Alzheimer's. He can't live on his own anymore."

"I'm sorry to hear that," Noah said. "How long are you going to be in town for?"

Matt tapped his finger against his glass. "I'm not sure, but since I don't have any court appearances scheduled until the New Year, probably until after Christmas. So, for the next three weeks at least."

Noah's eyes were steady on his face and Matt felt the vague urge to tell his friend the other reason he was in Boston. But talking wasn't something he found easy to do.

Noah didn't push, but changed the subject by asking another question. "So, are you going to contact DJ while you're in town?"

Matt sent Noah a sour look. "Who's asking, you or your fiancée?"

Noah grinned. "Jules's last words to me weren't

'I love you, you're such a stud,' but 'get Matt to tell you why he and DJ haven't spoken for nearly a year.'"

Matt shook his head. "You are so whipped, man."

Noah just grinned.

"I thought Jules and Darby would be happy to hear that DJ and I drifted apart. They aren't my biggest fans."

Noah rubbed the back of his neck. "Look, I'm in the middle here. I introduced you to DJ but I never expected your no-strings affair to last for years. I've told the twins to leave you two alone. You are adults and you both know what you are doing.

"But they love her and they are worried about her," Noah added.

Matt's head shot up. "Why are they worried about her?"

Noah released a soft curse. "You've got to know how much I love Jules, because if I didn't, I wouldn't ever consider broaching this subject."

Yep, whipped. If Matt wasn't the subject of the conversation, he'd find Noah's dilemma amusing. "The twins are worried because she hasn't been the same this past year. She's been quieter, more reserved, less…happy," Noah told him.

Matt filled in the blanks. "And they are blaming me for that?"

"Not so much blaming as looking for an explanation. DJ isn't talking, so my fiancée, damn her, asked me to ask you. Man, I sound like a teenager."

"So you didn't just accost me to have a beer?"

"The beer was an added incentive," Noah said, obviously uncomfortable. "Look, forget it, Matt. It's not my or Jules's business and I feel like a dick raising the subject."

Matt wanted to be annoyed but he wasn't. He'd always envied the friendship Dylan-Jane and the twins shared. They were a tight unit and would go to war for each other. He'd been self-sufficient for as long as he could remember, and his busy career didn't allow time for close friendships. It certainly didn't allow time for a relationship.

Matt carefully picked his words. "DJ and I have an understanding. Neither of us are looking for something permanent. I'm sorry if she's had a tough year but I don't think it's related to me. We were very clear about our expectations and we agreed there would be no hard feelings if life, or other people, got in the way of us seeing each other."

"Other people? Are you seeing someone else?"

Was Noah kidding? It had been a hell of a year and he hadn't needed the added aggravation of dating someone new. He'd had a slew of tough cases and he'd been sideswiped by explosive news and saddened by an ex's untimely death. And he was now required to make life-changing decisions for his once brilliant grandfather.

Starting something new with someone new when he was feeling emotionally battered wasn't the solution to anything. As a teenager he'd learned the

hard lesson that emotion and need were a dangerous combination.

He'd fallen in love at sixteen and he'd walked
around drunk on emotion. His ex, Gemma, and he
had made their plans: they'd graduate, go to college,
get married, have kids…and they'd feel like this forever. She was the one, his everything…

At seventeen she'd informed him she was pregnant. A part of him had been ecstatic at the news of
them having a baby—this would be the family he'd
never really had, his to protect, his to love. *His*. All
his…

After ten days of secret planning, and heart-to-heart
discussions, Gemma flipped on him, telling him she'd
miscarried and was moving across town and changing schools.

She didn't love him, she never really had…

He'd vowed then that love was a myth, that it was
a manipulative tactic, that it didn't really exist. His
parents, his grandparents, Gemma—they all proved
his point. At seventeen, he'd dismissed love and forever as a fabrication and nothing since had changed
his mind.

He now believed in sex, and having lots of it
safely, but love? Not a chance.

And sex, in his mind, meant DJ.

DJ didn't want anything permanent, either. Just
like him, she was allergic to commitment. They
spent just enough time together to enjoy each other

but not enough to become close. It was the perfect setup...

Or it had been.

He was back in Boston, in her city, and he saw no reason not to meet. It had been too long since he'd held her, since he'd tasted her skin, inhaled her fruity scent, heard her laugh. DJ, fun-loving, exuberant and sensuous, was exactly the medicine he needed. She'd be a distraction from thinking about how to handle the bombshell news he still hadn't wrapped his head around.

Matt looked at Noah. "I really don't know what's going on in DJ's life, but I doubt it has anything to do with me."

Noah drained his beer. "Are you going to see her while you're in Boston?"

Of course he was. "Yeah."

"Then I've been told to tell you that if you hurt her, they'll stab you with a broken beer bottle."

Matt rolled his eyes. DJ's friends were fierce. "Understood. But, as I said, we have a solid understanding."

Noah lifted his hands. "Just the messenger here." He pulled some cash out of his wallet and ignored Matt's offer to contribute. "If you don't want to spend the next month or so in a hotel, you're welcome to use the carriage house at Lockwood House. When we are home, Jules and I live in the main house."

Noah's property was, if Matt remembered correctly, the cornerstone of a very upmarket, expensive golfing community north of Boston. It was a generous offer and Matt appreciated it. "Thank you. That would be great."

"It was Jules's idea. That way she can keep an eye on you." Noah smiled. "And you do know that our house is directly opposite where Darby, DJ and Levi Brogan live? The same Levi Brogan who is superprotective and has no idea that you've been sleeping with the woman he loves like a sister for the last five-plus years?"

Oh, crap.

"It's going to be fun watching you tap-dance around him," Noah said before he clapped Matt on the shoulder and walked out of the bar.

Matt looked down at his phone and automatically stabbed his finger on the gallery icon. He flicked through the images of Dylan-Jane, memories sliding over him, and stopped when he came to a topless photo he'd snapped of her lying on the sand on a private beach in St. Barts. She was facing the sea but had turned her head back to look at him and the camera, her sable hair skimming the sand. She was all golden gorgeousness—flashing dark eyes, flushed cheeks, rosy nipples on her perky, tanned breasts.

Unable to resist her, he'd picked her up and carried her to the water, where they'd had amazing sea sex.

He had lots of great memories of DJ but, hell, making love to her in the sea and later on the sand was one of his favorites.

He desperately wanted to make more memories…

Shaking his head, Matt pulled up his last chat with DJ and quickly skimmed over the words they'd exchanged over the past week. He'd told her that he'd be in Boston the following week and asked if they could meet. DJ had sent him a surprised-face emoji as a reply...

Matt frowned. A surprised face wasn't a yes...

Neither was it a no...

What it was, was a strange way for DJ to respond.

She'd always been up-front and honest about telling him her plans, whether she could meet him or not. They didn't play games, didn't lie. They either wanted to be together, for a day or three or four, or they didn't. They could either make time for each other, or they couldn't. This year they hadn't managed to meet and that was just the way life went. He presumed she was busy managing her rapidly expanding design firm and he'd had his all-consuming work and the additional personal dramas to deal with...

But could she be dating someone else?

Matt's stomach tightened and he told himself to get a grip. He had no right to be jealous. They'd both agreed they couldn't expect to be monogamous when they were so far apart. He had been for the past year but that was more through circumstances than choice. They'd agreed to be honest with each other, to tell each other if someone else was on the scene. He hadn't had a text or phone call or email from DJ saying that. In fact, since late March, she hadn't reached out to him once. Previously, he'd received the odd email from her, funny memes that made him laugh, silly selfies she took.

Matt frowned, remembering that her friends were worried about her, that they thought something was wrong. Was she sick? Busy? Annoyed?

Or, worse, done with him, with what they had?

His phone beeped again and this time it was a text message. The distinct tone told him who it was from.

Hi. I'm not ready. Can I take some more time?

Sure, he replied. No pressure. I'm in town until after Christmas, unless something urgent comes up.

Right, he had no choice now but to wait until the daughter Gemma had never told him about decided to contact him again. And he wasn't visiting his grandfather until tomorrow.

So, what could he do with the rest of his day?

Mmm, maybe he could drop in to see Dylan-Jane. See whether there was a chance of them taking up where they'd last left off...

And, he admitted, he could see for himself whether she was happy or not.

In the coffee shop on the Lockwood Estate, Mason James delivered an espresso to the student sitting at the table in the corner and glanced at the complex math equation the kid was solving.

Because math had once been his thing, Mason

scanned the guy's rough notes and immediately saw where he'd gone wrong. Mason opened his mouth to point out the mistake before pulling back.

Three years ago, complex situations and equations, troubleshooting and problem-solving, was what he'd done for a living and he'd made a stupid amount of money from it. The responsibility of the problems he'd been given to solve—some of them with life-and-death outcomes—had generated enough stress to elevate his blood pressure to dangerous levels and burn a hole in his stomach. It had also ended his marriage and threatened his relationships with his sons.

So Mason got out of the think-tank business, buying a chic coffee shop to keep himself busy. He attended his boys' ice hockey and baseball games, played video games with them and helped them with their homework. He delivered coffee, muffins and pastries and told himself it was good to be bored.

Boredom didn't place a strain on his heart, or burn that hole deeper into his stomach.

Mason turned away and then heard the low curse. He looked around to see the student putting his head in his hands, tugging his hair in obvious frustration. It was, for him, simple math. What harm could it do to help?

Mason turned back, scanned the equation and tapped a line. "Rework this line."

Blue eyes flew up to meet his and Mason saw the doubt.

"With respect, I'm in the doctorate program at MIT..."

Mason shrugged and waited him out. He didn't bother to tell the guy that he'd been through that program and many more. He just tapped the line again until the kid finally turned his attention back to the equation. His brow furrowed and then he released a long sigh. Yep, the light had dawned.

"Hey, thanks so much."

Mason smiled briefly before retracing his steps back to his small kitchen. Before he reached his destination, he heard the muted ping that indicated he had a customer. He didn't need to see who was pulling the door open—his heart was way ahead of his eyes and it was already picking up speed.

Mason leaned his shoulder onto the nearest wall and watched his current obsession walk into his coffee shop, followed by a brunette clutching a stack of bridal magazines. The older of Callie's twin daughters, he remembered—Jules. Callie had her arm around Jules's waist and love for her child on her face.

Callie Brogan was a beautiful mom.

Mason ran his hand over his face. The last thing he was looking for when he opened Coffee Connection was to be attracted to a stunning, ebullient, charming widow. Yeah, she was older than him but who the hell cared? He could date younger woman, *had* dated many of them, and none of them captured his interest like Callie Brogan did. It was unexplainable and not something he could wish away.

God knew he'd tried.

Callie's head shot up and her eyes locked on his. Electricity arced between them and his pants, as they always did when she was in the room, tightened. Even though he was across the room, he could see her nipples respond—God, her breasts were fantastic. A flush appeared on her throat, down her chest. Despite her protests, Callie was as aware of him, as attracted to him, as he was to her...

Why hadn't they ended up in bed already?

Oh, because she wasn't ready and because she was still in love with her dead husband.

Mason looked up at the ceiling and shook his head. His was said to be one of the most brilliant minds of his generation, yet he was flummoxed by how to get this woman to sleep with him.

That's all he wanted, some fantastic sex with an attractive, interesting woman. He wasn't looking for love or forever—as a scientist, he didn't believe in either. The human species simply wasn't that evolved. But sex, a few hot nights? Yeah, he most certainly believed in man's most primal urge.

Mason started toward her—he couldn't stay away if he tried—but the infinitesimal shake of her head stopped him.

Right, he wasn't wanted. He should go and count stock or take out the trash or do his taxes.

Simple, stress-free jobs he could do with his eyes

closed. But so blah and boring. Looking through the huge windows of his shop, he wished he could go caveman on Callie. He'd toss her over his shoulder and put her behind him on his Ducati—in his fantasy it was spring or summer—and ride away. When he reached the first isolated area, he'd stop.

He had this fantasy of stripping her down, bending her over his bike and taking her from behind, his hands on her amazing breasts, his lips on her neck, sliding into her wet, warm...

"Sorry, sir? I'm stuck again. Could you help me?"

Mason rubbed his face before squinting at the messy calculations.

Since bike sex, or even warm weather, wasn't in his immediate future, he could do math. And while he mathed, he could also keep an eye on Callie, which was his latest and greatest pleasure.

Two

Matt walked into Brogan and Winston's showroom on Charles Street and looked around.

A counter ran along an exposed brick wall and to the right of it was a waiting area with a striped green-and-white sofa and a white chair, both with perfectly placed orange cushions. Funky art hung on the walls and a vase brimming with fresh flowers sat on the coffee table. He liked what he saw, immediately understanding why Winston and Brogan had such an excellent reputation and were booked solid for months.

DJ, as the CFO, worked behind the scenes, but Matt knew how important her work was to the company's overall success. He couldn't do what he did without Greta, his office manager, who took care of the paperwork, the staff and the billing. Greta was as indispensable to him as DJ was to Winston and Brogan. Her name, after all, was on the door.

Matt heard footsteps on the iron staircase to the left and he turned to see a pair of knee-high boots and sexy knees coming down the stairs. He knew those legs, the shape of them. He'd tasted the backs of those knees, nibbled those pretty toes. The rest of DJ appeared: short skirt over black leggings, a white blouse, that gorgeous long neck. As she hit the bottom stair, he finally got to see her face for the first time in too many months and, as always, her beauty smacked him in the gut.

Her thick hair, as dark as a sable coat, was pulled back into a soft roll, tendrils falling down the sides of her face. Black-rimmed glasses covered her extraordinary brown-black eyes and her lips were covered in a soft pink gloss. She looked both beautiful and bossy, efficient and exciting.

Two steps and she could be in his arms—he'd duck his head and he'd be tasting her.

"Matt."

No excitement, no throwing herself into his arms, God, he didn't even rate a smile? What the hell had happened between last Christmas and now?

Matt took a closer look at her eyes and saw wariness, a healthy dose of I-don't-need-this-today. Well, tough. He didn't like unresolved situations. When he'd left DJ in the UK everything had been fine. Yeah, many months had passed but, unless she now had a boyfriend and had moved on, nothing should've changed. And if she had found someone—a thought that froze the blood in his veins—then why the hell hadn't she just said so? That was their deal, dammit.

"Got someone else, Dylan-Jane?"

It took her a little time to make sense of his words, but when she did, her eyes widened and she quickly shook her head. Yep, that was answer enough. So, no boyfriend. "Then what's the problem?"

DJ glared at him, sent the young receptionist a cool smile and jerked her head toward the stairway. "Can we discuss this in private?"

Matt jammed his hands into the pockets of his pants as he followed DJ up the stairs and down a short passageway to a corner office. He stepped inside the brutally neat room and watched her stride toward her wide desk.

She wanted to put a physical barrier between them but he had no intention of letting that happen. One long step allowed him to capture her wrist. He swung her around and pulled her to him so that her breasts touched his chest and the top of her head brushed his chin. He looked down at her, his mouth quirking at her shocked expression. "So, no new guy, then?"

"No."

Thank God. Matt dropped his gaze from her eyes to her mouth and after a couple of beats, looked her in the eyes again. She immediately understood what he wanted…and yeah, it was what she wanted, too. The attraction between them had always been a living, breathing thing. A year ago, he would've dived into the kiss and been sure of his welcome, but too much time and distance had created a barrier between them. It was hell to wait for her to make the first move, to wait for her to rise onto her toes and fit her mouth against his. It took a minute, maybe more, but then her lips were on his and the world suddenly made sense again.

Matt immediately took control of the kiss, covering her mouth with his, sliding his hands over her hips and bringing her flush against him. His pants immediately shrunk a size as he filled the empty places of his soul by kissing Dylan-Jane. Spice, sex, heat, heaven…

It took less than a heartbeat for Dylan-Jane to open her mouth up to his tongue, and a second later her arms were looped around his neck and her fingers were in his hair. Potent relief ran through him: she still, thank God, wanted him as much as he craved her.

Matt wound his tongue around hers, tasting her spiciness and sweetness, and sighed. Yeah, he'd missed this, missed her breathy moans and the purrs of appreciation she made in the back of her throat.

When DJ's fingers pushed into his hair, when she held his head to keep his mouth on hers, he knew she was fully, completely in the moment with him.

Matt pushed aside his urge to strip her, telling himself that he wasn't going to make love to her on her office couch in the middle of the day. But he could kiss her, let her fill up those hollow spaces in his soul. He needed nothing as much as he needed to hold her...

Soft, sweet and still sexy—Matt felt like he'd conquered the world when she quivered under his touch. He needed to taste more of her, kiss a place more intimate than her mouth, so he flipped open the top buttons of her designer silk shirt and pushed aside the fabric to reveal her lace-and-satin bra. Unable to wait, he pulled aside the cup and there she was, pretty and plump. Ducking his head, he touched his lips to her, swiping his tongue across her nipple, feeling the shudder run through her.

He loved that he could make her feel like this, that he could take her from mad and sad to pleasure, that he could put those purrs in her throat, make her arch her back in eagerness. Her fingers in his hair tightened as he blew air over her nipple and his name on her lips was both a plea and a demand for more.

He moved to her other breast, loving the taste and texture of her. His hand traveled down her hip. Matt slid his other hand over her ass, kneading her under the fabric of her skirt before inching the material up so his fingers brushed the back of her thighs. He wanted those legs around his hips, her breasts in his mouth. He needed to be inside her as soon as possible.

He wanted them naked; he needed *her*. Matt's hand slid between her legs, wishing away the fabric barriers between her secret places and his fingers...

Then Matt was touching air and DJ was…gone.

Matt looked at the empty space between them and shook his head. One minute she was in his arms and the next she was halfway across the room, staring at him, her mouth wet from his kisses and her eyes blurry with desire. She wanted him, so why the hell was she six feet away and he was here? Matt took a step toward her and DJ held up her hands.

"This is my office, Edwards. I'm not about to get naked with you here."

Fair point. How soon could they leave? It had been a hell of a long time since he'd seen her naked, kissed her senseless, heard her moan as she fell apart in his arms.

"I'm not about to get naked with you at all."

Matt blinked. What?

There wasn't anyone else. They'd just shared a kiss hot enough to melt glass. They'd been sleeping together for many years. He was going to be around for the foreseeable future and she was cutting him off?

What was happening here?

What was he missing?

DJ gestured to the sofa. "Take a seat, let's talk."

He'd rather be making love, but since that was out of the question Matt sat down, adjusting his still rock-hard erection and begging it to calm the hell down because it wasn't needed at this precise moment.

"Coffee?" DJ asked.

Matt nodded, stretched out his legs and ordered himself to get a grip. He watched DJ with narrowed eyes as she popped a pod into her fancy machine, powered it up and, when the mug was full, added a dash of milk. Ignoring the sugar dispenser, she walked over, placing the mug on the coffee table in front of him. Then she took the seat opposite him and draped one slim leg over her bouncing knee.

DJ was nervous. Now, that was interesting.

"What are you doing back in Boston, Matt, and how long do you intend to stay?"

"I have some personal business that necessitates me sticking around for a few weeks. One part of that personal business is persuading my grandfather to move into an assisted-living facility."

DJ's eyes turned warm with sympathy and his heart stuttered. He loved her expressive eyes, the way emotions swam through them, the way they resembled luxurious chocolate.

"Is he sick?"

Matt shook his head. "Alzheimer's."

"I'm so sorry, Matt." DJ tipped her head to the side, curiosity all over her face. "And your other personal business?"

He wasn't ready to talk to her, or anyone, about his daughter, Emily.

Besides, he wasn't here to *talk*. He wanted to *feel*. He wanted to touch the skin on the inside of DJ's thighs, pull her tasty nipples into his mouth, nibble her toes. In her arms, while he loved her, he could forget about the complications of this past year.

Dylan-Jane was his escape, his fantasy woman, the perfect relationship because it was all surface. Because she didn't demand anything more than he was prepared to give.

But instead of falling into him and losing herself in the pleasure he could give her, she was retreating. Hell, if she had "back off, buster" tattooed across her forehead, her message couldn't be any clearer. DJ uncrossed her legs, leaned forward and rested her forearms on her bended knees. She stared at her hands for a long time before looking up at Matt. "Cards on the table, Matt?"

He didn't expect a good hand but nodded anyway.

"Your being back in Boston, even on a short-term basis, doesn't work for me."

Well, hell. Not what he wanted to hear. In his mind, reality crashed into fantasy and he felt a little sick. And a lot disappointed. He'd been relying on having some time with DJ as a way to step out of his head and regroup.

"I have a life here and that life doesn't have room for a hot lawyer who wants to share my bed." DJ glanced at her desk and lifted her eyebrows. "But maybe we can go somewhere in the New Year, see if the magic is still there."

Matt didn't know if she was being serious, and not knowing where he stood pissed him off. And there was something in her tone…something he couldn't put his finger on. Behind her tough-girl words, he could see vulnerability and...was that guilt?

"What aren't you telling me, DJ?"

DJ arched an eyebrow. "I don't know what you're referring to."

Damn if that prissy voice didn't make him harder than he already was, if that was possible. "Spill it, DJ."

Irritation flashed in her eyes and she shook her head, looking weary. "Lawyers. If you weren't so damn hot I wouldn't have hooked up with you." She sighed. "I don't have space in my life for an affair with you, Matt. I work long hours, I like my space. Also, I tend to get cranky around this time of year, so I prefer to be alone."

She didn't like Christmas? Why not? There was a story there. Another one. And why was he suddenly so curious? For seven years, he'd managed not to ask her questions, not to dig deeper, but now his first reaction to new information was to find a spade and start shoveling?

Get a grip, Edwards!

"Apart from a weekend of great sex with you here and there, I like being alone. Seeing you a couple of times a year is enough for me."

Matt leaned back, placed his ankle on his opposite knee and held DJ's gaze. She was trying so hard to remain calm, to persuade him that she was a cold woman who didn't feel anything, but she needed to become a lot better at lying before he bought into her BS. She wasn't cold, or sophisticated, or tough. What she was, was bone-deep scared of having him in Boston.

Why? Why could she easily handle a few days with him but seeing him regularly scared the pants off her?

And why did he care?

And why wasn't he saying to hell with this drama and walking out her door? He could leave, walk down the block and into a bar and, after a couple of cocktails and an hour or two of small talk, he was pretty sure he could score. But he didn't want sex with some random stranger.

There was only one woman he wanted...

Matt leaned forward and swiped his thumb across DJ's lower lip, his fingers lightly stroking her jaw. Desire burned in her eyes and under his fingers her skin heated. Glancing down, he noticed her nipples beading, pushing against the thin fabric of her silk shirt.

She'd never been able to hide her attraction to him, thank God. Because he saw her need for him, could feel her heat, could almost taste her...he pushed.

He kept his voice low, but his tone was resolute. "So here's what's going to happen, Dylan-Jane. I'm going to be living across the road from you and we're going to run into each other often. Your friends are mine and our paths *will* cross. And even if they don't, I'll make damn sure they do. It's been too damn long since I've had you and I want you under me as soon as possible. Yeah, this year has been unusual, I accept that. What I don't accept is this barrier you've flung up between us. But know this, I will pull it down and I will find out why you put it up in the first place."

"Matt—"

"Not done." He narrowed his eyes at her. "We've always been honest with each other and you're not being honest now. While I think part of what you said is true—you like being alone and Christmas sucks—that's not the whole truth."

"You haven't told me the whole truth about why you are back in Boston," DJ pointed out.

He hadn't, he had to give her that. "But that has nothing to do with you, nothing at all, and I know, don't ask me how, that your stay-away-from-me attitude is all about me, about us."

He saw agreement flash in her eyes and sighed. God, what was going on with her? And why couldn't she just spit it out? Matt closed his eyes and released a long breath.

"Jesus, DJ, just tell me already."

DJ stood up, walked over to the window and folded her arms across her stomach. She bowed her head and he could see her shoulders shaking. God, he hoped she wasn't crying. Tears were his Kryptonite. He stood up, went over to her and stood behind her, not touching her but silently offering his support. "You can tell me, Dylan-Jane."

DJ remained silent for a long time and when she

finally turned, he saw the capitulation in her eyes. Finally!

"We made love on Christmas Eve and I got pregnant." Her words were a series of punches in his solar plexus. He battled to find air, to make sense of her words. Then DJ took another deep breath and spoke again. "I lost the baby in February."

It took a minute, an hour—a decade—for his brain to restart, his mouth to work. He thought he was calm but when the words flew out of his mouth, they emerged as a roar. "Why the hell didn't you tell me? As soon as you knew?"

DJ's face drained of color and she retreated a step so that her back was flush against the window.

"I tried—"

"Not that hard," Matt shouted, unable to control the volume of his voice. "I had a right to know, dammit! How dare you take that away from me? You lied to me! You let me believe one thing when the exact opposite was true. Jesus, Gemma!"

Gemma? Had he really said that?

Matt stared at DJ, noting her dark eyes dominating her face. She was edging her way to the door, needing to walk away from him. He didn't blame her. In his anger and shock, he'd overlapped Gemma's and DJ's actions and he wasn't sure which situation he was reacting to. He needed to leave, to get his head on straight, to think about what she'd said, what had happened.

To find distance and control.

Matt whirled around, walked to the door and yanked it open. Stepping into the hallway, he saw Jules and Darby jogging down the hallway toward him with Amazonian warrior-woman expressions on their faces. They blocked his path, momma bears protecting their cub.

"What happened?" Jules demanded, her expression fierce.

"Did you hurt her?" Darby asked, equally ferocious. "If you hurt her, we will make her press charges."

God, what did they take him for? "She's fine. We just had an argument," Matt wearily replied.

Air, he needed air.

"If she's hurt, Edwards, I swear to God we'll string you up," Darby told him before she and Jules pushed past him and rushed down the hallway to their friend's office.

Matt watched them rush away, his heart trying to claw its way out of his chest. He rubbed his hand over his breastbone, trying to ease the ache, a part of him still not believing DJ's declaration. For the second time in his life, he'd heard that a woman had miscarried his baby. Unlike the last time he'd experienced this news, the baby he'd briefly given DJ would not, like Emily had earlier this year, write him a letter and tell him that he, or she, was his biological child and ask if they could meet.

He didn't want a family, wasn't cut out to be a dad, but, *man*, that thought made him feel profoundly sad.

Three

So wow. That happened.

DJ stared at her office door, flabbergasted by Matt's off-the-wall reaction. She'd spent hours imagining the conversation they'd just had, and she'd never once thought Matt—cool, calm, *controlled* Matt—would lose it.

And lose it loudly.

DJ dropped to the edge of her couch and placed her head in her hands. After trying to reach him a few times in March and failing to connect with him, she concluded that there was simply no point in telling Matt that she'd conceived and then miscarried. It had happened so quickly, he'd been so far away and, really, what impact would it have on his life? Zip. Zero.

If anything, she'd expected him to be thankful she wasn't still pregnant because, hell, a part of her was grateful for that.

There were many reasons why she felt relieved about losing the baby—and even more reasons why she felt guilty for feeling relieved. Not having to tell her own mother that she was going to be a single mom was high on the list. DJ hadn't had any contact with her father since she was a child, so telling him wasn't a factor.

Her parents were, in fact, the reason she'd never wanted to have kids. She was terrified that she, like them, would turn out to be as horrible at raising a child as they were.

She lived with the memories of her father walking away—at Christmas, for the love of God!—to move in with another woman and her child, a girl he adopted as his own shortly after leaving. He'd left DJ with Fenella, who wielded her tongue like a scalpel. DJ's goal in life had been to have an awesome career and enough money so she could be free from her mother's checkbook and caustic tongue. No stranger, DJ knew, could hurt you as much as someone you loved.

DJ's office door banged open and her best friends rushed inside. DJ stood, and Darby grabbed her biceps and gave her a tip-to-toe scan.

"We heard shouting. Did he hurt you? Are you okay?"

"What? No!" DJ frowned at them. "Matt would never hurt me."

Jules arched her eyebrows. "We heard him yelling."

DJ wrinkled her nose. Fair point.

"You don't fight, DJ, so what's going on?" Jules asked.

And there it was.

While she didn't volunteer information, she didn't lie to her friends. As Darby stepped back, DJ gestured for them to sit on the sofa. She'd dropped one bombshell today, she might as well drop another.

A year was a long time to keep this secret and now that she'd shared it with Matt, she didn't want to keep it to herself anymore. Darby and Jules were her friends, she should be able to tell them stuff. She *wanted* to tell them, even if it would be hard to say and, for Darby, hard to hear.

DJ looked at the twins, thinking that they couldn't be more different if they tried. Jules was dark-haired and blue-eyed, Darby a silver-and-steel-eyed blonde. The only thing they had in common was their stylish dress sense and the worried expressions on their faces. They sat down on the couch and Darby gestured to the chair opposite, silently suggesting that DJ join them.

DJ wanted to stay exactly where she was.

"Sit down," Jules suggested.

DJ touched her fingertips to her forehead, conscious of a monstrous headache. She sucked in some air, waited for her knees to lock and walked over to the empty chair, sending a wishful glance toward her coffee machine. Damn, she needed caffeine, preferably intravenously injected. And if it was laced with a stiff shot of whiskey, she wouldn't complain.

"Talk to us, DJ," Darby said, sounding worried.

DJ linked her fingers around her knees and tried to calm her racing heart. As a child, every time she'd tried to communicate with her mother, she'd been castigated, shamed or ridiculed. If she could avoid talking, she would. Because, when she tried to explain her thoughts and feelings, more often than not, she made a hash of things.

Look what a mess she'd made of talking to Matt. He'd stormed out, mad as hell.

Prior experience told her that this conversation wouldn't go well, either. DJ fiddled with her hair and sent a longing look toward her computer. This was why she liked numbers and spreadsheets and data. They didn't require her to form words.

"DJ, we're worried about you," Jules said.

"I'm f—"

"If you say you are fine, I swear I'm going to slap you!" Darby said, her words and expression fierce. "We know something is wrong, it has been for months and months!"

Hearing the fear and worry in her voice made DJ feel like a worm. And because she was already overly emotional, tears rolled out of her eyes and down her cheeks.

Jules dropped to her knees in front of DJ. "For

God's sake, just tell us already! Is your mom being a super bitch? Is it Matt? Did he do something to you?"

"No, that's not it." DJ ran her hand around the back of her neck and looked for her courage. Lifting her head, she looked past Jules to Darby. "This is so damn difficult for me, Darby, I don't know how to tell you this—"

"Just say it, DJ." Darby ground the words out.

"When Matt and I got together last Christmas, I got pregnant. I miscarried about six weeks later, in February. I never told Matt. I never told anybody."

Jules gasped, but DJ was most concerned about Darby. Color leached from her face and her bright eyes looked like moonlight in her face. DJ saw her friend's hands shaking. Just like she'd anticipated, Darby was taking the news badly.

DJ needed to apologize. "It was an accident. I didn't plan it. I knew it would upset you, so I didn't tell you. And I felt so damn guilty because I didn't want to be pregnant when you want a child so badly. And then I felt—still feel—sad, and guilty, for losing that child."

Darby rocketed up and slapped her hands on her hips. She shook her head and looked at Jules. "Can you believe this?"

Jules stood, too, and took a step closer to Darby, showing that they were a unit, a team of two, and that DJ was on the outside of their group.

"So, judging by his shouting, Matt is furious because you didn't share this news with him, either?"

When DJ didn't answer, Jules threw up her hands. "We don't blame him. He has a right to be as mad as all hell, Dylan-Jane."

DJ bit her lip. Okay, their reaction was worse than she'd expected. She lifted her hands and quietly murmured, "I'm sorry."

Tears turned Darby's eyes a lighter shade of silver. "I'm sorry that you had so little faith in us that you couldn't tell us sooner, DJ. I'm sorry that you think I am petty enough to only think about myself when you are faced with one of the most difficult situations of your life. I'm sorry that you think so little of our friendship, so little of yourself." Darby's soft words were loaded with sadness. They burned DJ like acid-coated hail.

"When are you going to realize that you can mess up, DJ, that you can be human?" Darby asked.

The hailstones turned into hot bullets that pushed through skin and bone to lodge in her heart.

"Dammit, DJ, for months we waited for you to talk to us, to ask us to share your burden. But you shut us out! Then you started looking and sounding better and you slowly started coming back to yourself, so we decided not to bug you, to let you be. But now we find out that you were pregnant and that you had a miscarriage and you chose to deal with all that alone?" Darby cried.

"Everyone was worried about you, DJ. Callie, Levi, the Lockwood boys," Jules added. "When are you going to realize that you are as valuable, as much a part of this family, as the rest of us? When are you going to start leaning, start accepting that we are here for you?"

DJ should trust them. She wished she could. They'd never, not once, let her down. But she was terrified that someday they might.

At eight, she'd believed she was the center of her dad's world, but he walked away without looking back. Her father had been the first, but Fenella continued the rejection. Every time she dismissed or denigrated DJ, played her mind games, DJ felt as alone, as abandoned, as she had the day her dad left.

It was easier to believe the people she loved would abandon her when she needed them most rather than face that kind of hurt again.

Darby rubbed her hands over her face. "Dammit, DJ, I am so sick of you trying to be perfect, of you standing alone and apart. I cannot believe I am saying this, but you have to make a decision. Either you are part of our lives in every way, prepared to lean on us, or you go your own way. Whatever you choose, we are never going through this again!"

This was the reason she didn't talk, why she kept her own counsel. Once again, she'd cracked open her shell only to have a knife shoved into her exposed belly. She talked to Matt; he'd exploded. She opened up to the twins, and they issued her an ultimatum.

"We need you to talk to us!" Darby said, her expression now determined. "We want to know about the big and the little things, the good and bad. And stop trying to find every excuse you possibly can for avoiding Christmas family functions. Enjoy being with us over the next few weeks. For the first time in your life, properly embrace what being part of our family means. If you can't do that, if you won't do that, then I think it's time we all move on. We love you too much to only have access to a facade. And frankly, we damn well deserve more!" Darby didn't raise her voice, but DJ was left in no doubt that she meant every word.

DJ looked at Jules, hoping to find her as shocked at this ultimatum as DJ. But Jules just looked sad. "Let us know what you decide, Dylan-Jane."

God.

Jules followed Darby to the door and when it closed behind them, DJ dropped to her chair and stared at the floor.

Yep, it was official. Having heart-to-heart conversations really wasn't what she did best.

The following evening, Matt walked across the road to Levi Brogan's house. Like most of the houses in the gated community, and like Lockwood House itself, it was Georgian-inspired with its portico and columns. But instead of redbrick, the cladding was painted a pale gray and the white-framed windows were free of shutters. Ivy climbed up the side of the three-story building and across the front of the three-car garage, on top of which was what looked to be a guest apartment.

Matt rested his hand on the gate and looked around. He liked this exclusive community, liked the amount of space between the houses, the big trees and the quiet streets. He was used to the bustle of city living in The Hague, but this golfing community held a serenity that appealed. He'd never visited here before.

This was Dylan-Jane's world, her people.

For years they'd met on neutral territory, places where neither of them had friends or acquaintances. They could focus on each other with no distractions. Their trips to unfamiliar places subconsciously reminded them that their time together wasn't real life.

But being in Boston, in her town, and living across the road changed that.

He couldn't get on a plane and distance himself. His obligations to his grandfather and the meeting he hoped to have with Emily were happening side by side with his need for DJ.

He wanted her—of course he did. He didn't think there would ever be a time when he didn't want her. But here, in Boston, he'd started wondering about more than the attraction between them. Which house was her childhood home? Had she climbed that magnificent maple down the street? Had she been a tomboy or a girlie girl, naughty or nice?

Matt rubbed his forehead with his fingertips, trying to push away the curiosity. He was asking for trouble if he looked at DJ as anything other than a no-strings, uncomplicated affair.

He didn't do complications. He avoided risk. For the past eighteen years, he'd forced himself not to think about having a family, reinforcing the belief that marriage and having kids wasn't for him. He'd been at the mercy of unpredictable parents and then unyielding grandparents and neither set of parental figures gave him anything near what he needed. He didn't want to perpetuate that dysfunctional cycle...

For eighteen years, he'd managed to stand apart, to not get involved, to be self-sufficient...but being in Boston made him think of family and those childish shattered dreams.

It had to stop. He was not an insecure kid anymore.

Enough of the past...

Matt jammed his hands into the pockets of his pants and rocked on his heels, still not walking through the gate. There could never be anything more between him and DJ, he knew that, but he was also certain that he owed her an apology. By losing his temper, he'd reacted badly. She'd shared a horrible experience with him and he'd seen the pain in her eyes, but he'd pushed her feelings aside to indulge in his life-wasn't-fair moment. He should've listened, tried to understand before reacting.

Yeah, not his proudest moment.

Irritated and ashamed, Matt pushed through the gate and walked up the steps to the ornate wooden door. He knocked and when a female voice answered, "We're in here," he stepped into the hall.

Matt followed the sound of the voice to a large sitting room filled with sofas covered in a mishmash of fabrics and colors. It shouldn't work, but it did. It was luxurious and comfortable and homey and chic all at the same time, and he immediately felt at home.

Glancing around, he saw Jules and Darby sitting on a flame-orange sofa, holding on to wineglasses like they were lifelines, tension radiating off both of them. Shoulders hunched, mouths tight, eyes bright. Matt frowned, looking for DJ. Where was she?

His big boots hitting the hardwood floor had them lifting their heads and he saw the misery in their eyes. Yeah, this wasn't good.

"What's happened? Where's DJ?"

Darby exchanged a long look with Jules and she released the breath she was holding. "Matt. Perfect."

A shed-load of sarcasm in two words. "Is DJ okay?"

"DJ is always fine, Matt, didn't you know that?" Darby said, her words bitter. But beneath the sarcasm, Matt heard pain and worry.

"She's in her apartment, Matt," Jules finally answered. "Yesterday and today were tough for her. If you were planning to keep fighting with her, please don't."

So Jules still felt protective of her friend. Her statement lessened one of the many coils squeezing his heart.

"Are you still mad at her?" Jules demanded, obviously curious.

No, his anger now had a different target—himself.

Matt shrugged. He wasn't in the habit of discussing his personal life, but these women were DJ's best friends, the people who knew her best. He kept his explanation short. "I've been calling her since last night. Messaging her, emailing. She isn't responding."

Darby shook her head, disappointed. "Join the club. God, I could just strangle her right now!"

Okay, so he'd obviously walked into some additional drama. Maybe he should come back later, when they were all a little more even-keeled. He was an expert at reading body language, but he didn't like dealing with drama anywhere other than in court, where he used it to get the result he wanted.

"What happened?" he asked, forcing a gentle note into his voice.

"I— She— DJ…grrr."

Matt lifted his eyebrows at Darby's actual growl. DJ had really managed to annoy the crap out of Darby.

Darby shoved a hand through her hair, looked from Jules to him and her chin wobbled. "Yesterday we gave her an ultimatum. It wasn't pretty." Darby threw up her hands and rapidly blinked. Yep, definitely tears. And damn, if she was in tears then DJ was more than likely crying, too.

Such fun. Matt sent a longing look to the door.

"I need to get out of here," Darby muttered, pulling at the collar on her white polo-neck sweater.

Since she made no effort to move, Matt figured she wasn't going anywhere.

But leaving sounded damn good and Matt wished he was anywhere else. Someplace that didn't have about-to-cry women, best friends fighting, a crap load of emotion. Nailing a bad guy using facts and words sounded like heaven right now.

"Maybe I should be the one to go."

"Yeah, you don't get to be that lucky," Jules told him, standing up. "The easiest way to get to her apartment is to leave the house via the kitchen door, turn right and the stairs to her apartment are there. Tell her that she's expected to join us ice-skating tomorrow evening. It's the first of our get-into-the-spirit events."

"Get into the spirit of what?"

A touch of amusement flickered in Jules eyes. "In the weeks leading up to Christmas, we all do fun things together. It's a tradition my dad started, and we've kept it going. DJ always finds an excuse to avoid any of our Christmas get-togethers."

"She does? I thought she loved hanging with you guys," Matt replied, confused.

Jules started to speak then looked at Darby, who shrugged. Some sort of twin-communication thing happened and Jules continued, "DJ gives a lot more than she takes. Despite a quarter of a century in our lives, she still doesn't talk to us. Maybe you being here can change that."

Matt saw hope flicker in her eyes and didn't like where her thoughts were taking her. It was better to shut down that line of thinking right now. "Please don't hop aboard the happy-ever-after train, ladies. DJ and I have an understanding that neither of us are going to go hearts and flowers on each other. That's not who we are, what we do."

Two sets of eyes were fixed on his face and Matt felt a bead of sweat roll down his temple. God, these women were tough. He tried again to get his point across. "Seriously, it's not going to happen."

Still nothing but intense stares.

Matt tested the words on his tongue, constructing sentences to convince them that there wasn't anything more between him and DJ than an inability to keep their hands off each other.

This isn't difficult, Edwards. Tell them you like DJ, you respect the hell out of her, but you have no intention of settling down with her, or anybody, ever.

DJ wasn't the problem—he was.

He opened his mouth to speak, but no words passed his lips. Great. He'd never, ever been tongue-tied before.

Another Boston first.

Mason saw, and ignored, the quizzical glances Callie sent his way as he sat at Eric's table, trying to help him grasp some of the trickier elements of partial differential equations. Judging by Eric's heavy sighs, Mason either wasn't explaining properly, or PhD-level math was a step too far.

Mason saw Eric's eyes flick to the intricate tattoo

covering the lower part of Mason's left arm and knew the kid was trying to reconcile his big brain with his hard-core tat. Eric would probably feel more comfortable taking instructions from someone not wearing cargo pants, biker boots and a black V-necked sweater, but...

Screw that. Mason had always marched to the beat of his own drum and it had been a long, long time since he'd felt the need to impress anybody, never mind a pimply-faced grad student. Cutting the kid loose with a suggestion that he take his problems to his math professor, Mason left Eric and focused on something far more pleasant. And difficult.

Callie Brogan was in the house and, as such, his day was made. Yep, it was official: he might look tough but his middle name was *pathetic*.

Callie saw him approach and looked from him to Eric and back again. He could see the wheels turning in her agile brain.

"What are you doing with Eric?"

Mason barely resisted running a quick hand over her bright blond hair. It would be soft and silky and he wanted it falling over his fingers as he plundered her mouth. But judging by Callie's inquisitive eyes, he was alone in that fantasy world. "Helping him with math."

"I've known Eric since he was a toddler and he's never needed help in anything academic." Callie frowned. "He's one of the top math scholars at MIT, so how can you help him?"

Thank God his ego was in decent shape or she'd have him whimpering. "I did have a life before this place, Callie."

"Doing what?"

"You haven't Googled me?"

"I prefer to get my information directly from the horse's, or in this case, the ass's mouth."

God, he loved her sass. "Come on a date with me and I might tell you."

Callie narrowed her gorgeous eyes and he fell into all that blue. He could easily imagine her naked on a deck chair on a golden beach, blue in her eyes, in the sea and in the sky. And wasn't that one of the items on her bucket list, to fall asleep naked in the sun? He could help her with that, but only after he spent an hour or two rocketing her to three or four of the most intense orgasms of her life.

Seeing that Callie was about to pepper him with more questions, he lobbed one of his own. "How far along are you with completing your bucket list?"

He'd heard that she went out on a date—not with him, dammit—and he was still pissed about it. "Had a one-night stand or phone sex yet?"

Callie flushed with either anger or embarrassment, possibly both. "That has nothing to do with you."

He saw the denial in her eyes and felt sweet relief. He was about to push for another date when Callie nodded to his arm.

"Did that hurt?"

Like a bitch but he couldn't admit that, so he

shrugged. Callie leaned forward to inspect the intricate Polynesian design. Her finger traced a raised vein on the outside of his arm and he felt a bolt of lust skitter along his spine.

Callie lifted her eyes and they slammed into his. "Do you have more?"

Oh, this was too easy. He grinned. "Maybe. Get naked with me and find out for yourself."

Callie made that sound that was half an embarrassed snort and half a laugh. He loved it.

Callie lifted her finger off his skin and he immediately missed her touch. Leaning back, she folded her arms and raised an eyebrow. "Are you doing anything on Friday evening? Around seven?" Callie asked him.

Mason didn't try to hide his surprise. "No, why? If you're about to ask me to a movie followed by dinner followed by sex, then my answer is yes, yes and hell, yes."

Callie rolled her eyes and Mason's mouth twitched. God, he loved annoying her.

"It's not, repeat, *not* a date but—"

He held his breath.

"—my clan goes ice-skating on the first Friday of December. Why don't you and your boys come along?" Callie suddenly looked doubtful. "Can you skate?"

It was his turn for an eye roll, but because he was trying to act his age, he resisted. "Sure, I can skate. Can I hold your hand on the ice?"

Callie frowned. "No, but you can tell me why you are so good at math."

"That knowledge is worth a kiss," he countered.

"On the cheek."

"With tongue."

"You're not that good and I'm not that curious!"

Mason leaned across the table, his eyes locked on hers. "Yeah, I am. And yeah, you are."

He was so close he could smell her coffee-and-mint breath, see the panic in her eyes. He looked down at her full, wide mouth before looking back into all that blue. Unable to resist, he dropped a kiss to the side of her mouth, not trusting himself to touch her lips. "See you on Friday, gorgeous."

"You are the most annoying, irritating, frustrating man alive."

Mason grinned and made himself walk away, knowing that Callie was watching his ass.

Yep, day definitely made.

Four

Matt tapped on DJ's door and when she didn't answer, he tested the lock, not surprised to find it open. Slipping inside her apartment, Matt waited for his eyes to adjust to the low light of the room. DJ took tidiness to the extreme.

The apartment was a showpiece, beautifully and expensively decorated, with cushions perfectly placed on the sofa facing him. The coffee table held a low vase with floating flowers, and a stack of magazines on the shelf under the glass top was expertly aligned. The desk in the far corner of the room was clean except for a slim, closed laptop and a black paper folder. The shelf behind her desk held a row of matching black files, each label immaculately printed. Nothing looked out of place—in fact, it barely looked like anyone lived in this showroom.

It was a far cry from the messy hotel rooms they'd shared over the past few years. Clothes were usually scattered over various surfaces—normally left where they tossed them—and towels ended up on the floor, with shoes where they could be tripped over. DJ had said she wasn't the same person at home as she was with him, and her apartment was the first evidence he had to back up that statement.

Matt made his way to a sofa facing a bay window that looked onto an icy pond next to a putting green. Nice view, he thought as he reached the back of the couch and looked down. DJ's eyes were closed and her even breathing told him she was asleep. Matt noticed the blotches on her face, the tear tracks on her cheeks, and sighed. He walked around the couch, looked down at another coffee table and decided that it looked sturdy enough to hold his weight. Sitting down, he rested his forearms on his thighs and looked at DJ. Really looked.

This was a stripped-down version of DJ, as natural and as beautiful as he'd ever seen her. Her hair was longer than before, her cheekbones more pronounced. The top button of her tailored white shirt had popped open, revealing the lacy edge of her bra and the swell of her breasts. Always so sexy…

Matt forced his eyes back up to her face. Beautiful, but even in sleep, she looked sad. God, had he done this? Her friends? Most likely it was a combination of both.

As if sensing him sitting there, DJ slowly opened her eyes. When he saw all that rich, deep, sad brown, his heart lurched. DJ lifted her hand and her fingers grazed his cheek.

"Matt."

Because he couldn't resist, he leaned forward and placed his mouth on hers, pushing his tongue between her lips. He tasted tears and wanted to burn them away, to remind her of the passion they shared that made everything else recede, if not disappear.

"Matt."

His name was a plea and a benediction, a cry and a hope. Matt kissed her again. This was what they were good at, what they needed. They weren't good at talking or connecting. But giving each other pleasure?

They excelled at that.

Sex was the best way to rebalance the scales, to take them back to that place where they felt comfortable with each other, to a time when their relationship was simple.

DJ placed her arms around his neck, lifting herself up so she was kneeling, her breasts pushing into his chest, her mouth nuzzling his neck.

Gripping her shoulders, he gently pushed her back, wanting to look into her face, into her eyes. Her gaze sharpened from sleepy to sexy and her voice, when she spoke, was rough with need.

"Kiss me, Matt."

It was the affirmation he'd been waiting for and Matt capitulated. His hands came up to tunnel into her hair, holding her head so he could thoroughly explore her mouth. His tongue twisted around hers and then he changed the angle of her head, looking to take the kiss deeper. He dialed up the passion from fiery to ferocious. DJ whimpered, held on to his shirt and made that low, growly, sweet sound that told him she was utterly turned on. When Matt pulled back to kiss her jaw, to suck her earlobe into his mouth, his hands got busy undoing her shirt.

"Hurry, Matt, I want you inside me."

"I haven't had you in nearly a year, there's no chance I'm rushing this." Matt's hands covered her breasts as he touched her through her silky bra.

Matt pushed aside the fabric and pulled one nipple into his mouth. He felt DJ's nails dig into his shoulders, the slight pain keeping him focused on his task of driving her insane before he pushed her over the edge.

Matt stood, banded his arm around her waist, lifted her off her feet and held her flush against his erection. How was he going to last? If she so much as brushed him with her hand, there was a good chance of it being over before he got to the fun stuff.

This woman made him lose control.

"Get naked," DJ panted, pushing his jacket off his shoulders. "I need to get my hands on your skin."

She yanked his shirt from his pants, pulling it up

his torso. While she explored his broad chest and dropped kisses on his hot skin, he reached behind and grabbed the collar of his shirt to pull it up and over his head. While he toed off his shoes and socks, DJ pulled off his belt and opened his pants. And finally, clothes gone, he was in her hot, soft hands. She circled him and rested her forehead on his chest, looking down. Matt gritted his teeth—he was so damn close—and dropped a kiss onto her dark head.

She was the only woman who could make him lose control. Needing her as mindless with sensation as he was, Matt got rid of her clothes, sighing at the little froth of red lace covering her mound. So feminine, so pretty, so DJ.

Matt pushed his hand beneath the tiny triangle to find her bead, blown away by how wet she was.

"You want me," he stated, his words coated with awe.

"I missed this, I missed you." DJ pushed her hips up, riding his fingers. "Come inside me, Matt. Fill me. It's been too damn long."

Matt knew she was close. Hell, he was, too, so he bent down to pick up his jacket, yanking his wallet out of the inside pocket. He found a condom, ripped open the packet and, with DJ's help, rolled it down his aching shaft.

Banding one arm around her narrow waist, Matt spread her legs so that her hips gripped his. He lowered them to the couch and she immediately slid over him, skin to sizzling skin.

DJ swiped her core over him before pulling him back with a gentle hand and positioning herself over his tip. He braced himself for the torture of entering her inch by inch, but DJ didn't wait, she just pushed down as fast and hard as she could.

She gasped, rocked once, twice, and he felt her insides contract, felt the rush of wet heat engulf him. Released by her orgasm, he launched his hips up, gritting his teeth as that familiar, white-hot sensation ran along his nerves.

He'd wanted to make it last, wanted to make DJ come again. He'd wanted to look into her eyes as she did…

He tried to hold on but when DJ ground down on him again, when he felt another tremor pass through her, he rocketed upward, his fingers digging into her butt, his mouth on her shoulder.

For a moment, for one single second as he shattered, he understood the way the universe worked, saw all the galaxies, rode a comet.

For one brief, blinding second everything made sense, and nothing was impossible.

As his heart slowed and his brain returned to its place between his ears, he heard DJ's ragged breathing, inhaled the intoxicating scent of her light perfume, soap and sex. His hand drifted up her spine, marveling at her soft, warm skin.

DJ slid her arms around his neck and pushed her nose into the underside of his jaw, her breath warming him. Matt started to speak but then realized that, once again, his tongue was tied.

How could he tell her that was the best sex they'd ever shared? That he felt more connected to her than ever before? That he couldn't imagine doing this with anyone else…?

Matt placed his hands on DJ's hips, easily lifting her off him and placing her on the sofa next to him. As he stood up, he felt her eyes on him, knew she was wondering why he so abruptly dislodged her.

Without looking at her—he couldn't afford to—he snatched up his clothes and stalked across the apartment to the guest bathroom. Closing the door behind him, he disposed of the condom, flushed and gripped the small basin.

He forced himself to look at his reflection, grimacing at the panic he saw in his eyes.

He *should* be panicked.

That wasn't fun sex or no-strings sex. It wasn't sex he could walk away from. That was crazy, want-to-do-it-again, want-to-do-it-again-for-the-rest-of-his-life sex.

Oh, God, he was in so much trouble. No.

They'd had sex. It wasn't a big deal. They'd had sex many, many times before. Nothing had changed.

Nothing. Had. Changed.

Everything had changed.

What the hell had she been thinking?

DJ kept her eye on the bathroom door as she

pulled on her clothes with jerky movements. She'd been half-asleep when she first became aware of Matt's presence and she wished she could blame her actions on her sleepy state, but that would be disingenuous, if not an outright lie. Matt had asked her whether sex was what she wanted and she'd been quick to agree.

It had, after all, been a very long time.

Sure, months and months had passed without any relief, but that wasn't why she'd said yes. No, her agreement was partly because she kind of, sort of, hoped that making love—no, having sex—would hit their reset button, that they'd magically be transported back to a time when getting naked didn't feel fraught with tension.

This time last year her relationship with Matt had been uncomplicated. They met, they made love, they left. Apart from a few days, a handful of times a year, their lives didn't intersect.

But now he was in Boston, in her life, living across the road. And, because she had terrible luck, he was here during December, which had to be her least favorite month, by a million miles.

DJ walked over to the window and looked down the road, noticing that most of the houses on the street were strung with Christmas lights. Levi intended to do theirs sometime soon and she'd heard Noah and Jules discussing how they intended to illuminate Lockwood House.

Every bulb, every colored light, every wreath on

every door reminded DJ of her father walking down the path to the sidewalk while she stood on the porch under twinkling lights and stupid mistletoe, sobbing while she begged him not to go.

She was rapidly approaching thirty. She should be over her antipathy to Christmas. It wasn't, after all, the holiday's fault that her father was a jerk. But as the lights went up and the nativity scenes, snowmen and reindeers appeared on front lawns, she felt her tension level ratchet up. By Christmas day, she felt ready to snap.

By adding a sexy human-rights lawyer who made her body sing, her heart sigh and her brain stutter to her Christmas angst, life was not playing fair.

DJ heard the door to the bathroom open and she turned to look at Matt. Like her, he'd dressed but his button-down shirt was open and untucked, and his feet were bare under the hems of his designer jeans.

He looked at home in her apartment. It felt right to see him here amongst her carefully collected possessions. DJ wondered what his place looked like, wondered if they shared the same taste, whether his furniture and art would jibe with hers.

Why was she even entertaining thoughts like these?

Matt was a fly-in-and-fly-out guy. And she liked that about him. She accepted that he wasn't the stay-still type and she knew she wouldn't be blindsided when he left her.

Because people always left.

Except the Brogans. And the Lockwoods.

DJ sighed. She'd spent most of her life protecting herself against the slim possibility that they might leave someday, too. But keeping herself apart had landed her in a heap of trouble and was at the heart of the current tension between her and the twins.

"Why the frown?" Matt asked her.

DJ jerked up her head to find him looking at her. Ignoring his question, she tipped her head to the side. "Why are you here? Why didn't you call before you came over?"

"I tried. Once or thirty times."

DJ remembered she'd turned off her phone after fighting with Matt and the twins, in an effort to find some much-needed solitude. She should turn it back on. "After you left, the twins and I had a disagreement about business, so I took some time to recharge."

Matt sent her a steady look. "I saw your friends on the way in. An argument over business wouldn't cause all of you to have red noses and wet eyes."

Dammit. He wasn't just a pretty face.

"Whatever you are fighting about is deep and personal and while a part of me wants to kick ass and take names, I'm going to assume you know how to fight your own battles.

"Besides, I'm nobody's white knight," Matt added, his voice rough. "Unless it involves statutes and penal codes and a check at the end of it, I'm not interested in saving anyone."

Yeah, she got the message: don't expect him to

run to her rescue. If she hadn't learned, a long time ago, that the only person she could fully trust was herself, she'd be disappointed.

DJ pushed her hair back from her face. "You never answered my question—why did you come by, Matt?"

She wouldn't insult him by suggesting that he'd only come over for sex because it seemed like he'd been as caught off guard at that happening as she'd been.

It was Matt's turn to ignore her question. "Have you got a beer?"

A drink sounded like a great idea. Why hadn't she thought of that? "Sure."

Matt followed her across the room, past the designer dining table to the kitchen area. He leaned his elbows on the counter and looked at her. "I never imagined your place to look like this, Dylan-Jane."

DJ frowned as she took a beer from her fridge and reached for a glass. "Like what?"

Matt shook his head at the glass she offered and took the bottle. "Minimalistic. So very luxurious but so damn tidy. I'm a bit of a slob but I thought you were even messier than me."

DJ leaned back against the counter and folded her arms. "I was on holiday, taking a break from being tidy. I told you, my time away from Boston with you was fantasy, and in my fantasy I don't have to be perfect."

"Who demands perfection from you?"

DJ turned back to the fridge, opened it and took her time removing a bottle of wine before reaching for a glass. She had no intention of answering that loaded question. When he didn't push, DJ turned around and poured herself some wine.

DJ looked up and met his eyes. "I suppose you want to talk about what happened."

"I'll listen to anything you want to tell me, DJ."

DJ gestured for him to follow her, leading him back to the sofa by the bay window. She tucked herself into the corner, bare feet under her butt, and gestured for him to take the other corner. Matt pushed the coffee table toward the window and stretched out his long legs. Moving down, he rested the back of his head on the sofa and they watched night shadows dance across the pond and putting green.

DJ kept it simple, briefly detailing the facts. A homeopathic medicine that, apparently, interfered with the efficacy of the pill. Initially thinking that she had food poisoning, followed by the dawning realization that she hadn't had a period for a couple of months. That carrying a baby was the emotional equivalent of being kicked by a horse.

"Why didn't you call me, DJ? Why go through that yourself?"

"I was taking it all in. I knew I should tell you but how to do that, what to say? There was nothing between us but a couple of weekends and some very hot sex and I suddenly had this child growing inside me, a child neither of us wanted, or was ready for. Then said child went away. End of story."

"Not hardly." Matt scoffed. "I would've listened, DJ."

But she didn't confide in others. She never had talked, not about her past or her childhood. What was the point of whining? Her childhood was over. She'd survived her father leaving and she'd survived being replaced when he adopted his new wife's daughter not even a year later. All communication between them ceased and DJ was down to one parent, Fenella, who possessed a brilliant mind and the personality of a honey badger.

Nobody saw the easily angered, frustrated and self-absorbed woman who'd raised DJ. In public, Fenella was affectionate and solicitous, but back home, she reverted to being mean and critical, constantly reminding DJ that she was nowhere near as bright, talented or accomplished as she needed to be. In Fenella's eyes, DJ was her only failure.

DJ lifted her eyes to look at him and when their gazes connected, attraction flared. Matt brushed his lips across hers and DJ sighed. The past faded, her tears were a dim memory and the argument with Jules and Darby, and their ultimatum, was forgotten. There was just Matt and the way he made her feel.

Physical contact was so much easier than an emotional connection. She felt his low curse on her lips before he pulled back, lifting his hand to push it through his thick hair. He took a long sip from his bottle while looking out the window into the dark, cold night.

"While kissing you is always a pleasure, I don't think it's a great idea right now. We both know we're not going to stop there and we'd be using sex as a distraction from this talk. Our attraction is still there, Dylan-Jane."

"As evidenced by crazy couch sex," DJ agreed. "Why can't we keep our hands off each other, Matt?"

"Possibly because we use sex to put a whole bunch of space between us, to avoid having deep, tough conversations."

DJ opened her mouth to argue before realizing that he was right. Deep conversation and swirling emotions weren't part of what they shared, who they were. She and Matt tumbled into bed, laughed through their love making, enjoyed each other's body. Their encounters had been laughter and tequila shots, room service and perfumed sheets.

They could never go back to that. Never again would she be able to call up Matt or send him an email with a link to an inn in Vermont or a castle in Scotland suggesting they meet. She'd never again meet him in a hotel lobby or wait for him at an airport, laughing as they rushed to make a connecting flight. She'd never sink into a Jacuzzi naked, her back to his chest, his leg wrapped around hers holding them in place.

The distance and events of the last eleven months had changed their relationship and they were now in no-man's-land. Despite the crazy couch sex, they couldn't be lovers again, but neither, despite this first meaningful conversation, were they friends. They were undefined, nebulous.

DJ didn't like undefined. Everything in her real life was carefully thought through, understood, slotted into boxes. At work she was brutally efficient, meticulous and detail-oriented. Even, as Darby and Jules frequently groused, anal. But the books were always balanced to the last cent, their returns were always submitted early, their creditors paid on time. She exercised regularly, had health and dental checkups every six months. Like her office, her apartment was ruthlessly organized, and her car was squeaky clean.

She had control over things but people baffled her.

Matt, the Brogans—they wanted her to communicate. They simply didn't understand that she didn't have it in her to exchange emotions on a deeper level. It was easier, safer, to retreat.

Or it had been.

Over the past year, things had changed. She'd changed. And now it was a few weeks off Christmas and Matt was here and suddenly she was feeling emotional connections she hadn't felt before.

She didn't know what to do with that.

DJ turned her head to look at Matt, watching as he rubbed the back of his neck. She wanted to replace his fingers with hers, tug his head down and kiss him. But she couldn't. They'd done it once, broken the drought, and they couldn't drink from that well again. Not here. This was the real world and in her real world she didn't get to kiss sexy men who weren't leaving town anytime soon. Because when her lover wasn't flying out the door, kisses led to dinners and sleepovers and breakfasts and more dinners and soon she'd be rearranging her entire life to keep him happy, to do anything to make him love her. She'd squash her own needs and feelings in the hope he'd love her like her mother never did.

So, no matter what she thought she was feeling, it was better to stay emotionally distant than to put herself in that position. She'd acknowledged and accepted that her parents had given her a warped view of love, but that wasn't something she could change. She simply sucked at relationships…evidenced by the fact that she might've messed up a twenty-five-year friendship.

"And the reason for that big sigh?" Matt asked, looking at her.

DJ shrugged and went for the easiest answer. "I'm trying to figure out how to mend my relationship with my two best friends. They are so mad at me."

"If it helps, I don't think they've totally given up on you. I was told to tell you they expect to see you at the rink tomorrow evening."

DJ groaned. "That's just cruel. They know I'm hopeless at skating." She was hopeless because she always made an excuse not to join the Brogans at the rink, to avoid their Christmas festivities and the memories that seemed to feed off carols and mistletoe, cookies and eggnog.

"I'm tagging along, too," Matt told her, his eyes glinting with amusement.

She wanted to smile, to lose herself in that warm green gaze, but she made herself take a mental step back. "Maybe it's better if we keep our distance from each other, Matt."

Matt held her eyes for a long minute, his gaze steady. DJ felt like he was looking into her soul, carefully taking her apart, piece by piece. When he eventually spoke, his tone was soft but full of purpose. "You and I are going to find a new way of dealing with each other and that starts now. I'm going to hold your hand and teach you to skate and we're going to try and be something we've never managed to be—friends."

Five

After Matt left, DJ sat cross-legged on her couch in the dark, her head in her hands. Damn, people confused her.

After years of wickedly hot sex and fun, uncomplicated weekends, Matt thought they should try and be friends… What the hell did that mean? That she should forget that he could send heat to her core with one smoldering look, a small brush of his hand against her skin? How could she be his friend when all she wanted to do was slap her mouth against his and run her hands over his broad shoulders? After all they'd done to each other, how could she be expected to shut off her attraction, to forget how he made her feel?

Yet, despite wanting to jump him whenever he

walked into a room, she couldn't allow herself to indulge. They'd taken the edge off, yes, but he wasn't here for just a night or a weekend. He would be here the next morning, the next day, the week after next. He was no longer her fantasy—he was here, part of her daily life, and she didn't know how to deal with that.

Matt's answer was to try something different: he wanted to be friends. But before she could make a new friendship, she had to fix the mess she'd made with her old friends.

After finding her phone, she quickly sent them a message.

Can we talk? Fifteen minutes, in the kitchen?

They both responded in the affirmative and DJ sucked in a panicked breath, feeling her heart rate accelerate at the thought of opening up. She told herself she didn't need to fear their reaction. If they got angry, they wouldn't disparage or demean her. They'd only ever shown her love...

She could do this. She *had* to do this.

Not giving herself any more time to think, she picked up her phone and dialed Callie's number.

"Baby girl." Callie answered the call the same way she'd done all her life. DJ felt her heart stammer, then settle. This woman had been, in so many ways, her rock and her sounding board, an untapped source of unconditional love.

"Hey, Cal."

"What's wrong?" Callie demanded, her voice sharpening. DJ could imagine her leaning forward, her mommy instincts on high alert. They'd never been able to get anything past Callie.

"Nothing is wrong but I do need to talk to you. And the twins."

Callie hesitated. "Scale of one to ten?"

It was a throwback to her childhood. Callie was the mom all the kids gravitated to for advice. She'd developed a system to filter teenage nonsense—one to three meant the news wouldn't matter in three months' time, four to seven meant it was marginally important and eight to ten was life-changing.

DJ sighed. "Twelve?"

Callie was silent for ten seconds before speaking again. "I'll be there in five."

Just like that, no questions asked. DJ disconnected the call. She slipped on her coat, shoved her feet into the old boots she kept by her front door and stepped into the night. Frigid air burned her throat and made her eyes water as she walked down the stairs to cross the lawn and head up the broad steps that led to the kitchen door of their magnificent house.

While she'd grown up in a house possibly even more luxurious than this one, this Georgian-inspired building was home. DJ looked left, saw Levi's SUV parked to the side of the garage, knowing that their expensive sports cars and Levi's imported superbike were tucked behind doors of the four-door garage.

They lived a privileged, wealthy life—they had all the tech and toys—and she was grateful.

But as she'd learned, money just helped paper the cracks on a life; it didn't plug them. Money didn't shield you from pain.

DJ left her coat and boots in the mudroom and slipped into the lavish gourmet kitchen to see the twins entering the large, airy space from the hallway. Without saying a word, Jules reached for three wineglasses and Darby selected a bottle of French wine. DJ watched them, thinking that a warm glass of red would go some way to soothing her jitters.

"Your mom is on her way," DJ quietly told them and saw their eyes sharpen. Neither of them spoke. Jules just retrieved another glass and Darby poured wine into crystal goblets. Silence prevailed until Callie burst through the back door, shrugging off her cashmere coat and pulling her gloves from her fingers with her teeth.

"What's going on and what did I miss?" she demanded, flinging herself into a chair and reaching for a glass.

Looking at Callie, DJ wondered how the woman could ever call herself old or fat. Yeah, she wasn't stick-thin, and neither did she look like she was in her thirties, but she was still one of the most attractive women DJ had ever laid eyes on. Fenella was coldly beautiful, her features perfectly aligned, but Callie was arresting in a way that Fenella was not.

Callie was warmth and charisma, a big, bold personality who oozed love and natural charm.

No wonder Hot Coffee Guy was, as DJ had heard, flirting with her.

Jules tapped DJ's hand to pull her back to the present, a place where she really didn't want to be. *Suck it up, cupcake.* Yeah, it might feel like a root canal but what was the alternative? Losing the twins? Not an option.

Ever.

Three sets of amazing eyes looked at her and DJ pulled in a big breath. Releasing the air, she looked at Callie. "I've been keeping quite a big secret from all of you." Right. Another big breath. "At the beginning of the year, I miscarried Matt's baby."

Callie's eyes radiated sympathy. "Oh, baby. I'm so sorry."

"I'm sorry I didn't tell you what I was going through," DJ said, keeping it simple. "I should've." DJ pushed her hair behind her ears. "I didn't tell you because I was trying to protect Darby—" she saw Darby wanting to interject but DJ held up her hand, asking for patience "—but I know that was just an excuse."

"And what does that mean, DJ?" Jules asked.

DJ bit the inside of her lip. "It's easier to keep things inside, to bury them deep. I'm not good at… exposing myself. I'm not good at friendships." DJ saw that they were all about to protest and raised her hand again to keep them from interrupting. "I'm not, but I'm going to try and do better. I have to get a handle on this friend thing, partly because you said so."

Jules raised an arched eyebrow. "Only partly?"

DJ pulled a face. "And also because that's what Matt and I are trying to be."

"He friend-zoned you?" Darby asked, amused.

"It was a mutual decision." DJ darted an embarrassed look at Callie. "After this last year, things just feel *different*. We couldn't go back to what we were, so we thought we'd try something new."

Jules laughed. "That is too funny. You can't possibly be friends with someone who sets your panties on fire. But it'll be fun watching you try."

Then Jules touched DJ's hand with the tips of her fingers, her expression turning serious. "We'll talk about that man again—and dear Lord, he's so much sexier than I remember!—but I have something to say first."

Oh, dear. They were going to let her off the hook, of that DJ was reasonably certain, but not without a hell of a lecture first.

"DJ, you are the most independent woman we know, and that's saying something because we're pretty damn independent, too," Jules said quietly. "Your loyalty to us is absolute. Whenever we've needed you, you've moved mountains to be there. You are happy to give, but it's time you realize that you have to take, too. You not leaning on us, not reaching out to us—it had us worried. But you also hurt us."

"We know that you find it difficult to talk—"

Difficult? No, impossible!

"—but you cannot keep isolating yourself, pulling back into your shell when life slaps at you. Life is a series of ups and downs but your I-can-manage-on-my-own streak stops here and it stops today." Jules's gaze pinned DJ to her seat. "Are we clear?"

DJ nodded. "Does your ultimatum still stand?"

She needed to know. She couldn't live her life with that over her head.

Callie frowned as Darby and Jules exchanged long, guilty, remorseful looks. "We were mad at you and we wanted to get your attention. We would never really walk away from you, I hope you know that," Darby admitted.

Callie's eyes narrowed. "You threatened to walk away from her?"

Jules and Darby squirmed in their seats at their mom's displeasure. Jules wrinkled her nose as she explained, "As Darby said, we were mad at her."

Callie's eyes were ice-cold. "The problem with knowing each other so long and so well is that you know exactly what buttons to push to inflict the most hurt. Threatening to walk away from DJ was cruel and I am *not* happy."

DJ wriggled, feeling uncomfortable. She never imagined this conversation would turn into Callie fighting with her daughters. Dammit! Look what happened when she talked.

"Mom, DJ knows it was just a way to make her see the light!" Darby protested.

"By threatening her with her greatest fear? Her dad walked away at Christmastime and Fenella frequently threatened to do the same thing! She often told DJ that her father had the right idea, that DJ wasn't good enough or smart enough or pretty enough for her father, or Fenella, to want to stick around."

Darby pushed her chair back and ran around the table to wrap her arms around DJ, resting her head against DJ's. "I'm sorry, DJ, I didn't think!"

DJ patted the arm that was choking her and when Darby released the pressure against DJ's throat, she sucked in some air. When she felt like she could breathe again, she kept one hand on Darby's arm and, with the other, took Jules's hand. "It's okay. And you were right to be mad. I should've opened up to you. I really should've."

"Damn right you should've," Callie tartly retorted.

DJ nodded. Underneath Callie's frustration was a lifetime's worth of love and DJ knew how lucky she was to have these amazing women in her life, standing in her corner.

It was hard to say the words, but she needed to…

"I love you," she said, her voice cracking. She waited a beat before speaking again. "That being said, do I still have to do the Christmas thing?"

"Yes!" Callie and Jules and Darby said in unison.

Well, crap. It had been worth a shot. Darby released DJ and went back to her chair as Jules replenished their glasses. A comfortable silence fell over the table for a few minutes before Darby spoke again, lifting her eyes to meet DJ's. "Can I be honest?"

"When are you ever not?" Jules murmured.

"Am I jealous that you got pregnant accidentally? Hell, yes. Did I have a moment of 'it's not fair'? Absolutely, I did. And I think that's normal," Darby stated, her voice low.

DJ couldn't think of a response so she remained quiet as Darby continued. "But those are *my* emotions, what I have to deal with. I know that you two will have babies eventually. Sometime in the future, one of you will carry a child and I'll be grateful to walk beside you, experiencing it, even if it's only secondhand. When it happens, I want to be involved. Please don't shut me out."

DJ leaned across the table to wipe Darby's tears off her cheek, unaware that her own tears were flowing as freely.

The back door opened and they turned tearstained faces to see Levi walking into the room, his T-shirt streaked with grease. He stopped, looked from one face to another and then walked across the room, yanking sheets off the roll of paper towels. Having grown up with their tears, he didn't bat an eyelash as he tipped up chins and wiped away their tears.

When he was done, he tossed the soggy sheets in the trash can and placed his hands on his hips. "Wine, tears, holding hands. Whose ass needs kicking?"

* * *

Matt had faced down hardened criminals and sly lawyers, hard-assed judges and tough police officers, and not once had he felt nervous or out of his depth. He had the law on his side and he knew how to bend it to get the outcome he wanted. And, not to blow his own horn, he was damn good at it.

But now, as he lifted his hand up to knock on the Brogans' wide wooden door, he felt jittery.

He'd received a message from Dylan-Jane, inviting him over for dinner, and he was still deciding whether to knock. Matt wasn't good at family occasions; his experience with family meals had been an extreme of opposites. Meals with his parents had been people sitting around makeshift tables drunk or stoned or both, with little to eat. Meals with his grandparents had been filled with food, but were stilted, boring affairs, where nothing but law and politics were discussed.

His daughter, the one he still hadn't met, had grown up with better family dinners than he had. From her emails, he gathered that Emily's family was close. She had two younger brothers, also adopted, a houseful of pets, a successful dad who adored her and a stay-at-home mom. Matt was so grateful that she'd had a stable, loving home to grow up in.

He'd experienced poor and unstable. He'd experienced rich and stable. But in both situations, he'd been only tolerated and mostly ignored.

Yet here he was, standing on another doorstep,

about to face another family. And as if that wasn't hard enough, he also had to keep his burning attraction to DJ under wraps.

Yeah, he'd spouted off about being friends, but... God, he was feeling anything *but* friendly. How could he be DJ's friend when all he wanted to do, all he thought about, was exploring that sexy mouth, running his tongue down her neck, over the slope of her perfectly shaped breasts, and pulling her puckered nipple into his mouth? He wanted to hear her gasps of pleasure on his lips, on his skin. He wanted to swallow her whimpers of delight, hear her soft panting after he pushed her over the edge.

Forget being her friend. He'd far prefer, on any day, to be her lover. After many years of phenomenal sex, he now had to stand in the friend zone?

What the hell had he been thinking?

"Matt."

Matt turned and saw that the front door was open, that DJ was waiting for him to step inside. After hanging up his coat, Matt scanned her face. Her olive skin held more color than the last time he'd seen her, but her enormous, brown-black eyes dominated her face.

He'd always loved her eyes. They were the first feature he'd noticed seven years ago. That night she'd had no makeup—she didn't need any—and worn tight jeans and a tighter top. Their eyes had met and his heart, young and stupid, bounded out of his chest and flopped at her feet.

Just like it was doing right now. Dammit.

Tonight, her jeans were designer, with strategic rips, and she wore them with a simple long-sleeved red T-shirt. Simple clothes for a meal at home, but she looked as sexy as a red-carpet diva. Slender bare feet ended in flame-colored toenails and the denim fabric lovingly caressed her long legs and the gentle flare of her hips. He pulled his head back to glance at her ass and…crap. Yeah, fan-friggin'-tastic.

Again, just how was he supposed to keep his hands off her?

DJ held out her hand for him to take. Spontaneous gestures of affection weren't DJ's style, but Matt took her hand and laced his fingers in hers, frowning as a tremor ran from her to him. She looked up at him and smiled hesitantly. "Hi."

Resisting the urge to kiss the hell out of her, he dropped a kiss on her temple and murmured in her ear, "Are you okay?"

"Much better, thanks," DJ replied, her voice soft.

"Did you speak to your friends?"

Her hand rested on his chest and she grabbed his shirt as if to hold on. Under her hand his heart was beating hard. "Yeah. It went better than I thought. We kissed and made up, but they refuse to let me ignore Christmas."

"One of these days you are going to tell me why you hate Christmas," Matt murmured.

"If you tell me why you're really in Boston," DJ countered.

She looked up at him, her eyes begging him to tell her the truth. He knew it was partly curiosity and partly because she was feeling off balance at having opened up to him. She probably thought that if he told her his own truths, then some of the balance of power between them would be restored. But he couldn't.

He'd promised Emily and, more than that, he couldn't afford to become any more emotionally intertwined with Dylan-Jane than he already was. He was leaving in a few weeks and, God willing, in the New Year they'd go back to fun weekends, hot sex and casual goodbyes. They couldn't move from friends back to lovers if they allowed their thoughts and feelings to bubble forth in Boston.

Hot sex, fun weekends—that was what they did. Matt frowned at the bitterness he tasted in the back of his throat at the thought that he might want more.

What the hell was wrong with him?

"Edwards."

Matt turned around and looked across the hallway to where Levi Brogan stood, arms crossed and a serious look on his face. He had rich brown hair, and his stubble held a hint of red. With cold eyes and a belligerent attitude, Brogan radiated enough aggression to ignite a turf war. Matt instinctively knew Levi was not a man to be messed with.

Levi walked across the hall and yanked open the front door. Ignoring DJ, he jerked his head toward Matt. "Outside."

Ah, crap. Matt sensed movement behind him and turned to see the three Lockwood men stepping into the hall. Levi's hot glare stopped their progress. Levi held up his hand and shook his head. "Nope, just him and me."

DJ moved in front of Matt. "Levi, stop being a jerk! This has nothing to do with you."

God, she was trying to protect him? Seriously? Matt felt a warm glow in his stomach before he realized that she was putting herself between two big men. Not a place for a small woman to be.

"Move, Dylan-Jane," Matt commanded, holding Levi's hot eyes.

"No! This is insane. You are not Neanderthals!" DJ cried. Frustrated, Matt placed his hands on her waist, easily lifted her and sat her butt on the edge of the hall table, not caring that it was obviously old and very valuable.

"God, you definitely need to eat more," Matt muttered. Ignoring Levi and the sharp eyes of the Lockwoods, Matt placed his hands on either side of her thighs and waited until her eyes, deep brown and worried, met his. When was the last time someone had worried about him? He couldn't remember. And why did he feel like his heart was being warmed by a gentle fire?

"Levi is protective. He might punch you," DJ whispered.

Matt swallowed his smile at her obvious concern. "I know. I can handle him."

"I don't want you to fight," DJ said, biting her lip.

"We're big boys, Dylan-Jane, and hopefully it won't come to that." His words failed to reassure her so he shrugged and compromised. "I promise I won't throw the first punch."

"You men are ridiculous."

"I know." Matt dropped a kiss on her nose and straightened. Without looking at her again, and ignoring Noah and his brothers, he walked through the open front door and onto the wide porch to face Levi. Matt placed his hands in his pockets and waited for Levi to speak.

"When I got home, the three of them were in tears."

Since Levi failed to ask a question, Matt didn't bother to answer him. It was a lawyer thing.

A minute passed with Levi not saying anything and Matt became tired of waiting. "If you are going to punch me, can you get it over with?"

Levi's head jerked up and Matt caught the smallest flicker of amusement. "I don't know if you could handle me punching you, lawyer boy," Levi taunted.

"Yeah, that's what the last guy I put down said," Matt replied, keeping his tone light.

Levi folded his arms across his big chest and his biceps bulged. Yeah, the guy was bigger than Matt, but not by much, and Matt was fast and sneaky. He'd hold his own.

He hoped.

Levi nodded. "So, what's the plan of action?"

"I'm not sure what you are asking me, Brogan."

Levi looked annoyed, but Matt suspected that annoyed might be his default expression. "I don't like the idea of you dropping in and out of DJ's life."

"What DJ and I do has nothing to do with you or your family."

Levi glared at him. "Of course it does! From what I can work out, for the first couple of years this thing you had seemed to work. She still dated and we met a few of the guys she was seeing—"

A red haze appeared in front of Matt's eyes at the thought of DJ seeing other men. Over the past seven years he'd never once worried about her sleeping with anyone else. Why now?

"But then she stopped. We all flirt and have fun, she doesn't. I feel—we all feel—like you are playing her, stringing her along, keeping her at your beck and call."

It galled Matt to have to explain himself—he wasn't the type—but this was obviously a major concern for DJ's friends. He needed to address it so he could enjoy his meal with them. "I don't know what to say to you, Levi, and I wish I did, because I would love this conversation to end. All I can tell you is that DJ and I have an agreement."

"Great sex and no commitment?"

It was a mutual, adult decision and Matt had nothing to be ashamed of. "Yeah." Frustrated and wanting to go back inside, preferably without a broken nose, Matt sighed. "I like and respect DJ. She knows that.

I'm pretty sure you heard about the miscarriage and I'm not discussing that, except to say we are trying to work out how to deal with each other going forward. I don't want to hurt Dylan-Jane and I'll do the best I can to make sure that doesn't happen. That's all I can promise you."

Levi rubbed his hand over his beard, nodded once and held out his hand. "Levi Brogan, protective big brother."

Matt gripped Levi's hand. He assumed the interrogation was over, but then Levi clasped Matt's shoulder and dug his fingers into his muscles. Matt forced himself not to react to the ribbons of pain running down his arm. "Let's go have a beer."

Matt allowed Levi to take a step or two toward the door before shaking his arm out and rolling his shoulder. The man had skills and he was very thankful that big fist hadn't connected with his face.

Not having to deal with protective big brothers and friends was just another reason not to bother with commitment.

But it had felt nice, earlier, to have DJ defending him, and he liked knowing that if he wasn't around, DJ had some good guys looking out for her.

Walking into the hall, Matt ignored the thought that *he* was the guy who should be looking out for her.

Six

Mason James walked between his sons and scanned the familiar sight of Frog Pond, Boston's favorite ice rink.

He'd been bringing Emmet and Teag to skate at the famous landmark since they could stand, and despite their feigned nonchalance, he knew his boys loved the bright Christmas lights and the festive atmosphere at the rink. Mason, skates over his shoulder, looked from one young face to the other. Time passed so damn quickly. Within a year or two, his house would be empty. No shoes on the floor, sports gear in the hall, or messy bedrooms, no having to constantly restock the fridge.

He'd be alone.

He'd miss his boys, of course he would, they'd

been a band of three for a long time, but being alone didn't scare him. Being bored did. And while the coffee shop was a nice change of pace, it wasn't what he wanted to do for the rest of his life.

He was still figuring out what that might be.

Helping that kid with math had been a rush, an unexpected pleasure. He'd forgotten how beautiful equations could be.

It was the first time in a long time that he'd admitted that he missed his old life, missed the satisfaction that came with solving complex problems. He didn't want to go back to the stress, but he couldn't see himself making coffee until retirement.

This was his town; MIT had been his playground. His work at the think tank and several patents had paid for a few houses, lots of big-boy toys and a fat bank account. He was fit, healthy, youngish— he could do anything and go anywhere. He needed adventure. And definitely more sex.

Maybe that was why he was so drawn to Callie.

She challenged him on a level he'd never experienced before. Breaking through to her was proving as hard to solve as string theory.

Mason released a long sigh and two heads turned to look at him with bright, inquisitive eyes. "Problem, Dad?" Emmet asked.

"I'm good."

Like he was going to explain to his teenage sons that he was having woman problems. They spent enough time obsessing about girls without adding his own drama to the mix.

Speaking of, he looked around for a curvy blonde, wondering if Callie had conveniently forgotten her invitation to meet him here. Maybe she was running scared again and hiding from their attraction. He was so damn over it.

He wanted her, she wanted him… It shouldn't be complicated.

"Skating would be a lot better with a stick and a puck." Teag was Mason's hockey-mad offspring.

"Yeah, but then there wouldn't be any pretty girls," Emmet replied as they approached the rink.

Mason watched as Emmet made eye contact with a girl a year or two older than him, saw his flirty look and the lift of his head. The blonde nodded to the rink, sent him a see-you-on-the-ice-big-boy look and Mason's stomach tightened. Oh, God, he was going to have to repeat the make-smart-decisions-and-always-wear-a-condom speech. Talking to his oldest about having responsible sex, when he wasn't having any sex at all, was a special type of torture.

"Mason?"

Lust skittered up and down his spine and blood rushed from his head straight to his groin. Not feeling much older than his sons, Mason slowly turned to look into Callie's bright eyes—her blond hair was under a woolen cap that covered her ears. Her nose and cheeks were red, her coat was a bright pink and her tight jeans showed off her great legs. Her skates were a bold, bright green and she looked as at home on the ice as she did on land.

"Hey."

He heard Emmet's snort and knew the kid was rolling his eyes at Mason's greeting. After jamming his elbow into Emmet's side, Mason gestured to his sons. "Meet my monsters, Teag and Emmet. Boys, this is Ms. Brogan."

Teag mumbled a hello but Emmet held out his gloved hand and smiled. "Ms. Brogan. Nice to meet you."

Any other father would've been proud of Emmet's show of manners but Mason knew his son was a born flirt and could charm any female from birth to a hundred and ten. It was his superpower.

Callie shook his hand. "Nice to meet you. You boys skate?"

"Yeah, they skate. I've been bringing them here since they were tots."

"And by middle school he couldn't keep up," Emmet teased.

"Like hell." Mason rolled his eyes at Callie and smiled in response to her grin.

She looked so young standing there, with her unpainted mouth and flushed cheeks. It took all he had not to lean across and cover his mouth with hers, to see if her lips were as cold as he thought.

Mason pulled his wallet out of his jeans pocket, took out some cash and handed it over to the boys.

"Go and buy us some tickets. I'll meet you at the entrance."

"Trying to get rid of us, Dad? So we won't embarrass you in front of the pretty lady?" Emmet queried, laughing.

"You embarrass me on a daily basis," Mason responded, knowing his boys wouldn't take his words seriously. He worked damn hard to make sure they knew he loved them and was proud of them. "But yeah, go find someone else to bug."

Teag rolled his eyes and Emmet laughed again. Tossing a quick goodbye to Callie, they melted into the crowd. Mason turned to Callie, putting his hands over Callie's as they gripped the railing. "Will you still be here when I get back?"

Callie lifted a finely arched brow. "Do you want me to be?"

"More than you'd believe," Mason fervently replied.

"You don't want to hang with your kids?"

"Even if I did, they don't want to hang with me. And they weren't joking about being able to skate rings around me." Mason ran his finger down Callie's cheek, frustrated at not being able to feel her through his leather glove.

So he pulled off the glove and cupped her cold face in his hand. Better, so much better. His hand covered the side of her face and he pushed the pad of his thumb onto her bottom lip.

He couldn't resist—he needed a taste, just one. He

lowered his head but Callie's hand on his chest kept him from connecting. "Mason, your boys might see you kissing me!"

"I'm pretty sure they won't pass out from the shock."

Callie lifted her aristocratic nose. "Public displays of affection are not my thing."

Mason swiped his thumb across her bottom lip again before releasing her with a deliberately loud sigh. "So I guess my fantasy of parking off a side road and taking you from behind as you lean over my Ducati isn't going to happen?"

Callie's mouth fell open. She flushed but Mason didn't miss the way her eyes turned a deeper blue… with lust? Interest? Curiosity? Well, now…

Then Callie narrowed her eyes at him. "What do you want from me, Mason?"

It was a good question and one he could answer honestly. "Sex. A couple of laughs. Some conversation. More sex."

"I'm not looking for a relationship, Mason. That's not what I want. Or need."

Mason dropped an open-mouthed kiss on her temple and whispered in her ear. "I'm not asking you for one, Cal."

With the colored lights and laughter reflected in her eyes, she looked damn perfect, like his own personal Christmas angel. He pulled back, fighting his instinct to brush his lips across hers, to burrow under her bright jacket to cup her breast.

God, she was driving him mad.

Callie pulled away and skated backward. She smiled at him—genuinely—and his heart flipped over in his chest. Mason was surprised that it could still do that.

"Hurry back, Mason, and I'll show you that I can skate rings around you, too."

He released a short burst of laughter. "Big talk, Brogan!"

Callie spun into a pirouette and Mason watched her spin faster and faster until he felt dizzy. When she came to a stop she was neither out of breath nor wobbly.

"Show-off," Mason grumbled, unable to keep an impressed smile off his face.

"Ten minutes, or else I'll find someone else to skate and flirt with," Callie told him, her expression saucy. He loved her laughing eyes, her wide mouth, the energy vibrating off her. Soaking her in, he just stared at her, unable to get his feet to work.

This was the woman he wanted to spend time with, the one he was completely captivated by.

Callie patted her head and touched her face with her gloved hands. "What's wrong?"

"Nothing. You are just so damn beautiful that you take my breath away."

Callie's face softened, her eyes misted over and her lip wobbled. God, he hadn't meant to make her cry. He'd spoken the truth. It had been wrenched from deep inside his soul.

Crap, why was his soul forcing words out of his mouth?

He'd spoken the truth not two minutes ago. This was pure lust. There was nothing here his soul needed to be concerned about.

He'd tried commitment, monogamy, marriage. It wasn't a road he was interested in walking again.

Callie spun around once and when she stopped, her eyes were clear as she tapped her watch. "Eight minutes. You're running out of time."

Mason bolted. There was no way he was missing out on his chance with the most intriguing woman on the ice.

DJ walked onto the ice at Frog Pond and felt her feet slide away from her. Gripping the railing, she swallowed her curse and tried to get her balance under control. DJ lifted her head up and looked around.

Noah and Jules were skating together, hand in hand, while Darby skated in front of them, shamelessly showing off her skill. Levi, Ben and Eli were behind them, looking as at home on the ice as they did on the boats they loved to sail.

Where was Callie? DJ's eyes moved across the pond and she saw her standing on the far side of the rink, talking to… DJ narrowed her eyes. Was that Hot Coffee Guy? *Go, Callie.*

DJ tried to turn around so she could face the skaters—she really wanted to watch Callie flirt with Mason—but her feet wanted to go south in-stead of east. Cursing, she stayed where she was and continued to look around. Despite her aversion to anything Christmas, the brightly colored lights decorating the trees surrounding the ice rink looked fantastic. Blue, red, green, yellow and pink were draped through the trees and the café was brightly adorned with white.

She could—almost—see the appeal. With one hand DJ tugged her beanie over her ears before push-ing her nose into her scarf. She'd left a spreadsheet incomplete at work in her rush to get to the rink. Not because she wanted to skate, but because she knew Matt would be here.

DJ wanted Matt with an intensity that made her breath hitch and threatened to buckle her knees. She had his scent—sandalwood and spice—in her nose and she could easily picture his broad hands, mascu-line and powerful. Then she imagined those hands on her body, in her hair, between her legs.

Maybe she'd conjured him up, because suddenly Matt was flying across the ice toward her, stopping with pinpoint precision in front of her.

DJ got an impression of dark jeans, a caramel-colored coat and a red beanie before his bare hands cupped her face and his hot mouth covered hers. DJ gripped his coat with one hand, sighing into his mouth when his kiss gentled, exploring, tantalizing. His thumb stroked her cheek and she tasted mint and coffee and sex and sin, a heady combination that had her releasing her grip on the railing.

Her feet shot out and she felt herself falling, her legs flying between Matt's as they both tumbled to the ice. DJ felt air leave her body as her tailbone and then her back collided with the ice. Whatever oxygen she had left whooshed out of her when Matt fell on top of her.

Matt immediately placed his hands on the ice and pushed himself up, his arms holding his weight off her. "DJ? Honey? Are you okay?"

DJ opened her mouth but no sound came out and she snapped it closed. She tried again and...nope. Nothing.

"You're winded, honey," Matt said, rolling off her and kneeling on the ice. "Sit up and take slow, deep breaths. You need to stay calm and relax."

Yeah, easy for him to say when he wasn't the one who couldn't breathe. Matt pulled her up, held her face and looked in her eyes. "Breathe for me, Dylan-Jane. In and out, there you go."

DJ felt air hit her lungs. With every breath she took, she relaxed a little more.

When she could, she spoke. "Ack, talk about sweeping me off my feet, Edwards." DJ held out her hand so Matt could pull her up. He grabbed her hips when her skates went haywire again.

"Technically, you swept me off my feet," Matt said, wrapping a strong arm around her waist. DJ sank against him, knowing he wouldn't let her fall.

DJ looked around for the exit. This skating ma-
larkey wasn't for her. "Can you guide me off the
ice, Matt?"

Matt leaned against the side of the rink, pulled
her between his legs and gripped her with his knees.
With his hands steady on her hips, she felt stable. He
was so close, their breaths mingling in the cold night
air, and DJ thought about reaching up to kiss him
again, but then remembered that was what caused
their fall in the first place.

Really, she shouldn't be thinking about kissing
him at all. Weren't they supposed to be *friends*?

She groaned and Matt, because he was so in tune
with her, sent her a sideways look and a half smile.

"It's hell, isn't it?" he asked.

"What is?"

"Wanting each other so much. I look at your mouth
and remember the way you taste. I keep looking at
your hands, wishing they were on me...stroking me."

She had to ask. "Stroking you where?"

Matt pulled her hand under his coat and placed
it on his crotch. She felt the beginning of what she
knew would turn into a fantastic erection.

A fireball of lust rolled down her spine and lodged
between her legs as Matt allowed her hand to drop to
her side. One comment! One small innocuous comment, a quick feel and she was turned on.

DJ darted a look at Matt's profile, frowning at his
having-a-pleasant-time expression. So unfair that he

could look calm and controlled while her face was on fire and her panties were one spark from igniting.

Yeah, some payback was in order.

DJ sent him what she hoped was a seductive smile. "I keep thinking back to St. Barts. You looked mighty good handcuffed to that canopied bed." She felt the tension in Matt's back, heard his ragged intake of air and smiled. "If I recall, I only used my mouth."

Matt muttered something under his breath that sounded like a series of creative curses. DJ smiled at the pained expression on his face.

Scales rebalanced... Now he was as turned on as she was.

"This is our first time out together as *friends* and ten minutes into the conversation we're in the bedroom," Matt complained.

"You started it by kissing me," DJ retorted.

"You started it by looking sexy and confused, trying not to enjoy the Christmas lights and decorations, trying to resist the festive atmosphere."

Dammit, he was so perceptive.

Warmth seemed to radiate off him so she shuffled her feet forward and gripped the belt loops on his jeans. "And then we kissed and you went up in flames."

His grip tightened on her hips. "What are we going to do about it, Dylan-Jane? I can't help thinking that, after all we've done together, the sexual shenanigans in St. Barts included, trying to be your friend is the most dumb-ass suggestion I've ever made. Tell me you want me as much as I want you."

"Matt—"

"Is that a yes, a no…a hell-I-don't-know?"

"All three," DJ whispered, looking up. "We haven't even *tried* to be friends, Matt!"

Matt sighed. "I know. But I also know that the first time we are truly alone, all our clothes are coming off."

That was the truth.

He met her eyes, both of them oblivious to the fact that kids were chasing each other across the ice, that lovers were gliding arm in arm, that a Santa and his elves were doing figure eights in the center of the rink. DJ lost herself in his gaze and wished they were alone, that they were naked and that he was sliding into her, completing her.

"I want you, DJ. Only you."

Dammit, Matt! DJ wrenched her eyes off him and sucked in some cold air. If she didn't think she'd land on her butt again, she'd skate away.

She had to be sensible, just for a minute. She needed clarity. "Where are you going with this, Matt? Are you saying we should sleep together?"

Matt nodded. "I can't think of you as a friend. I certainly can't treat you like one. So, for as long as I am here, let's do what we do best. We can think of our time together as just being another weekend, but…longer. And when I leave after Christmas, we kiss each other goodbye and go back to normal."

Could she do this? Could she mix her real life and her fantasy life by having a fling with Matt? Would that be a solution to the yearning and churning, constant craziness she felt whenever he was around?

C'mon, Dylan-Jane.

She was kidding herself if she thought this would be like their weekends away. He was in her town, watching her live her life. Here in Boston, he couldn't be her fantasy man, she couldn't pretend her real life didn't exist. This *was* her life and he was standing smack in the middle of it.

Reality dictated that they couldn't spend every moment together making love, they'd have to talk more, spend nonbed-time together. And that was dangerous. One of the reasons she limited her time with Matt was because she liked him, a lot. He had a wicked sense of humor, a razor-sharp brain and streaks of honor and integrity a mile long.

He could tempt her into wanting more than good sex, into thinking about commitment and relationships and belonging to someone.

And wanting that from a man, looking for love, was a sure way to get her heart diced.

She'd experienced heartbreak when her dad left and knew what it felt like to be left behind. And thanks to her mother, she also knew what it felt like to love someone who didn't love her back. She didn't want to relive either experience.

But most of all, she didn't want to fall in love.

So don't, she told herself. *Just don't.*

"Are you going to put me out of my misery sometime soon?"

She should say no, but she wasn't going to. Going to bed with Matt, having an affair with him, was pretty much all she'd been thinking about since he'd dropped back into her life.

"Yes, okay. Let's have a fling." Not able to look at Matt, DJ sent a longing look toward the café, its lights beckoning her to come in and get warm. "Well, let's go, then. Your place or mine?"

Matt chuckled. "I want you, Dylan-Jane, but a few more hours won't kill us. Let's teach you to skate and then we can join your family out on the ice."

DJ looked to where Matt pointed and she saw Darby and Jules skating together, arm in arm. Noah held Jules's other hand and Callie, sans Hot Coffee Guy, had her hand tucked in Levi's elbow. And they were skating toward DJ.

Jules and Darby were the first to reach her and both sent her a concerned look. "We saw you fall. Are you okay?"

"I'm fine. I just really suck at skating."

"You really do," Matt agreed, his arm still holding her upright. DJ rolled her eyes. She knew that. Hell, they all knew that.

"Let's get off the ice and get a table, then we can all be together," Darby suggested, but DJ heard the reluctance in her voice. They all loved to skate and if it wasn't for her they'd be on the ice for another hour at least.

"No, you guys carry on," DJ told them, tightening her hold on Matt. "Matt's offered to catch me if I fall."

Darby lifted her eyebrows. "You sure?"

DJ nodded. "Very. What about meeting in an hour? I'll buy the first round."

Her clan chorused their approval of that suggestion and skated off. DJ watched them go, love and affection bubbling in her chest.

God, she loved them. All of them. Feeling a little overemotional, she tipped her head back to look at Matt, whose eyes were on her face, his expression tender. Not ever having seen that look from him before—a combination of pride and affection and lust—DJ bit the inside of her lip. He couldn't—*shouldn't*—look at her like that. It not only made her want to strip him where he stood, but it also coated her heart in warm goo.

No acting gooey, stop with the mushy thoughts.

This would be just a series of sexual encounters over the next month or so. She was not going to let it be more than fantastic sex with someone she liked.

Really liked.

A *lot*.

DJ pushed back her shoulders, ignored her wobbling ankles and tried to put a cheeky smile on her face.

"Let's do this." she said, her tone jaunty.

"Yes, let's."

Instead of helping her with her uncooperative feet,

Matt curved his free hand around her neck, placed his thumb under her chin and tipped up her head. His mouth hovered over hers, his words dancing on her lips. "We'll skate, but right now, let's do *this*."

Matt's green eyes scanned hers then lingered on her mouth before he pulled his gaze back up to meet hers. Eye contact, DJ decided as electricity skipped over her skin, was damn sexy. His thumb, slightly cold, grazed the side of her face, across her cheekbone, toward her ear and back again. Anticipation sizzled.

Instead of using his lips, he moved so that his cheekbone skated across hers, skin on skin.

DJ muttered his name before tilting her head so that her lips brushed his…once, twice…and silently demanded to be kissed. Masculine lips touched her cold ones and DJ was instantly plugged into a source of heat warming her from the inside out. Tongues circled, danced, withdrew and tangled as she and Matt stood on thin blades in the freezing night, oblivious to the background music of Christmas carols and the hoots of skaters.

Maybe December and Christmas—the decorations, the lights and the festivities—weren't as bad as she'd always thought. But honestly, she was kissing Matt, which meant anything and everything was instantly bolder and brighter and better. Even Christmas.

"FAST FIVE" READER SURVEY

Your participation entitles you to:
✳ 4 Thank-You Gifts Worth Over $20!

Complete the survey in minutes.

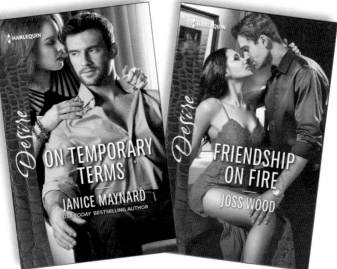

Get **2 FREE** Books

See inside for details.

Dear Reader,

Since you are a lover of our books, your opinions are important to us... and so is your time.

That's why we made sure your **"FAST FIVE" READER SURVEY** can be completed in just a few minutes. Your answers to the five questions will help us remain at the forefront of women's fiction.

And, as a thank-you for participating, we'd like to send you **4 FREE THANK-YOU GIFTS!**

Enjoy your gifts with our appreciation,

Pam Powers

To get your
4 FREE THANK-YOU GIFTS:

✴ Quickly complete the "Fast Five" Reader Survey
and return the insert.

"FAST FIVE" READER SURVEY

1 Do you sometimes read a book a second or third time? ○ Yes ○ No

2 Do you often choose reading over other forms of entertainment such as television? ○ Yes ○ No

3 When you were a child, did someone regularly read aloud to you? ○ Yes ○ No

4 Do you sometimes take a book with you when you travel outside the home? ○ Yes ○ No

5 In addition to books, do you regularly read newspapers and magazines? ○ Yes ○ No

YES! I have completed the above Reader Survey. Please send me my 4 FREE GIFTS (gifts worth over $20 retail). I understand that I am under no obligation to buy anything, as explained on the back of this card.

225/326 HDL GM3T

FIRST NAME

LAST NAME

ADDRESS

APT.#

CITY

STATE/PROV.

ZIP/POSTAL CODE

HD-817-FF18

READER SERVICE—Here's how it works:

Accepting your 2 free Harlequin Desire® books and 2 free gifts (gifts valued at approximately $10.00 retail) places you under no obligation to buy anything. You may keep the books and gifts and return the shipping statement marked "cancel." If you do not cancel, about a month later we'll send you 6 additional books and bill you just $4.55 each in the U.S. or $5.24 each in Canada. That is a savings of at least 13% off the cover price. It's quite a bargain! Shipping and handling is just 50¢ per book in the U.S. and 75¢ per book in Canada*. You may cancel at any time, but if you choose to continue, every month we'll send you 6 more books, which you may either purchase at the discount price plus shipping and handling or return to us and cancel your subscription. *Terms and prices subject to change without notice. Prices do not include applicable taxes. Sales tax applicable in N.Y. Canadian residents will be charged applicable taxes. Offer not valid in Quebec. Books received may not be as shown. All orders subject to approval. Credit or debit balances in a customer's account(s) may be offset by any other outstanding balance owed by or to the customer. Please allow 4 to 6 weeks for delivery. Offer available while quantities last.

◄ If offer card is missing write to: Reader Service, P.O. Box 1341, Buffalo, NY 14240-8531 or visit www.ReaderService.com ►

BUSINESS REPLY MAIL
FIRST-CLASS MAIL   PERMIT NO. 717   BUFFALO, NY

POSTAGE WILL BE PAID BY ADDRESSEE

READER SERVICE
PO BOX 1341
BUFFALO NY 14240-8571

NO POSTAGE
NECESSARY
IF MAILED
IN THE
UNITED STATES

Seven

DJ opened the door to her apartment and stepped inside. The living-room drapes were open, and she immediately noticed the soft white lights strung up over Lockwood House, softening the austere lines of the two-hundred-year-old home.

DJ took off her coat, hung it up on the stand next to the door and walked over to the window facing the street. "Lockwood House looks pretty."

Matt moved to stand behind her, his arms banding her waist, his right hand covering her left breast in an action that was as familiar as it was exciting.

Matt rubbed his chin across her head. "By the way, doesn't anyone in this neighborhood believe in colored lights?"

"Noah's grandfather, and great grandfather, only

ever used white lights to decorate Lockwood House, and the tradition has extended to all the houses in the community."

"It seems like a nice place to live," Matt murmured.

"It really is. A community of its own." DJ tipped her head to the side so Matt had better access to her neck. God, she loved the way he used his tongue and teeth.

DJ reached down, found the switch to her lamp and warm, golden light filled the lounge. This wasn't a hotel suite, she suddenly realized. Those were her books on the shelves. She'd chosen the painting above the mantel, the glass bowl on the coffee table.

This wasn't neutral territory, this was her home. And Matt was in it and he was about to make love to her.

He was in her space again…in her very intimate, feminine space. If he left—when he left!—she'd have memories of him here, in her bed, naked in her apartment. She didn't know if she wanted that, but then again, she couldn't stop this…

Well, she could—of course she could. Matt would walk away if she asked him to, but she didn't want to ask him anything.

Except, maybe, to inquire as to when he was planning to strip her down and kiss her in certain feminine, neglected places.

Matt pulled her sweater up and over her head. DJ felt the clasp of her bra spring apart. Then the material was a flash of blue on the floor and Matt's

tanned hands were on her pale flesh, kneading and
squeezing her breasts, her nipples pushing into the
palms of his hands.

DJ felt Matt step away from her and she turned
around to watch him pull his shirt and sweater over
his head, revealing a wide chest lightly covered with
sun-kissed hair. His happy trail, darker and heavier,
ran from his belly button and disappeared beneath
the band of his jeans.

DJ's hand drifted over his stomach, her fingers exploring the hard ridges of his six-pack. How he managed to maintain his fitness level and physique while
working the crazy hours he did, God only knew.

"Bedroom," Matt commanded, holding out his
hand.

Darby led him up the stairs into the loft, wondering if he'd like her bedroom, decorated by Jules Brogan in cream and mint.

But Matt only had eyes for her—his gaze moved
from her breast to her face and back again as he
shucked his shoes and stepped out of his jeans.

Moving around her, he lay down on the bed and
tucked his arms behind his head. "I love watching
you undress."

The appreciation in his expression, the desire in
his eyes, made her feel intensely feminine, extraor-
dinarily powerful. DJ took her time, slowly removing her boots, sliding her leggings down her hips
inch by excruciating inch.

When she was finally naked, she sat down on the

side of her bed, her hip pressing into Matt's hard thigh. Her thumb skated over his hip bone, and she marveled at how soft his skin was right there. Holding her hair back with her hand, she bent down so her lips could graze his shaft, her tongue could nibble his tip with tiny, sexy touches she knew he loved. She felt him jump, go from simply hard to steel, and wasn't surprised when Matt's hand gripped her head, urging her to take him into her mouth. She did, and twisted her tongue around his tip, curling her fingers at the bottom of his erection.

She used her mouth on him for a few minutes more before sliding up his body, straddling his hips so that her core came into contact with his solid heat. She was so close already, it wouldn't take much...

"This. You." Matt lifted his hands to play with her breasts, then lifted himself with his core muscles— hot, hot, hot—and swiped his tongue across one nipple, then the other. Holding himself in that position, he slid a finger between her and his dick, finding her happy spot with deadly precision.

"Need you, baby," Matt muttered, falling back. His other hand patted the side table and he lifted the foil packet to his teeth, ripped it open and pulled the condom from the packet. Sliding her back, he rolled down the latex, his eyes glinting with desire.

DJ wished they could make love without a condom. She wanted to feel him skin on skin, heat on heat. She thought about suggesting it, but knew he'd never trust her again. She'd failed them once when it came to birth control and he wouldn't take another chance. She didn't blame him, but a part of her wished they had that level of trust.

Matt placed his hands on her hips, pulled her so the tip of his penis rested at her opening. She expected him to slide in—she was wet and ready and he knew it. But Matt just pulled her head down and gave her a long, languid kiss before his eyes, so brilliantly green, looked into hers.

"What are you thinking, DJ?"

She couldn't tell him. It was too personal, far outside the parameters of what they expected from each other. She pulled a smile onto her face and rubbed herself against him, still resenting the thin barrier between them. "Just thinking how much I enjoy this and how much I love being with you."

"A truth but not the whole truth. Tell me, Dylan-Jane."

DJ rolled her head, looking toward the window to avoid his eyes. Matt gently turned her head to face him again. DJ saw the determination on his face and knew he wouldn't let this go. He was going to stay exactly where he was until she told him the truth. Dammit.

"I was wishing that you trusted me enough to go without the condom, so we could be together without a barrier." She saw the flash of panic in his eyes and shook her head. "I understand why you won't and I don't blame you… It would've been nice, that's all," she quietly added.

Matt didn't say anything but his eyes didn't leave hers. She felt his hand slide between them, felt him touch himself before pulling his hand away again. Before she could comprehend that he'd removed the condom, he was inside her, skin on skin, his heat and hardness filling her, touching her without any barrier between them. Igniting instantly, she surged against him, blown away by how splendid he felt.

But mostly, she was conscious of her heart swelling, her soul sighing at his display of faith. Tears ran down her cheeks and she buried her face against his neck, feeling absolved and trusted. And if she allowed herself the fantasy, this one action of his might suggest that she was loved. Just a little.

At the thought, an orgasm slammed her hot and hard. Her heart and soul detonated simultaneously.

Mason tossed back the comforter on his bed and sent an uninterested glance at the massive flat-screen TV on the opposite wall. He sat down on the edge of his king-size bed and looked at the pile of books on his bedside table. He didn't want to watch TV; he certainly didn't want to read. What he most wanted was Callie…

He wanted her here in his cream-and-brown, professionally decorated bedroom, rolling around on his big-enough-for-a-party bed.

He ran his hand over the back of his neck, feeling like his skin was too tight for his body. After skating, he should be tired, but what he needed was a release, an hour or two—or five—of unimaginable pleasure. Mason picked up his phone and scrolled through his contact list, stopping when he hit a name. Kate would be awake; he could call, slip out of the house and be at hers in twenty minutes.

It was very late, his guys were asleep and a nuclear bomb would have trouble waking them up. They would never know he was gone. Mason looked down at his T-shirt and his thin cotton pants, and knew that he wasn't going anywhere. He didn't want Kate.

He didn't want anyone but Callie.

Crap. Mason dropped his head and released a series of f-bombs, cursing his attraction to a woman who filled his thoughts and haunted his dreams. Once he got her out of his system, his life would go back to normal, he was sure of it.

Mason looked down at his phone and scrolled up, stopping on the Cs. Her number was there, big and bold, taunting him to call. If he couldn't see her, taste her, make love to her, then he could hear her voice.

Mason glanced at the time, saw that it was close to midnight and sighed. She'd be asleep and she wouldn't appreciate a midnight call...

But what if she wasn't? What if she was up and thinking about him and feeling lonely and horny and frustrated and...

What if she was feeling even a little of what he was?

No guts, no glory.

Mason hit the green icon on his phone and held his breath as the phone dialed out. One ring, two.

Four, five…crap. Mason was at the point of hanging up when Callie's breathless "hello" stopped the incessant ringing.

He was so surprised that, for an instant, he lost his words.

"Mason, if you're trying to do some heavy breathing, you're really bad at it."

Mason chuckled. "Sorry, I didn't expect you to answer so I zoned out from surprise."

"Why wouldn't I answer?" Callie asked.

"Sleeping, annoyed that I phoned you so late," Mason replied, leaning against his leather headboard. He swung his legs onto the bed and closed his eyes, allowing the slight rasp of her voice to slide over him.

"I seldom go to bed before twelve thirty. And I'm happy you called me."

Mason smiled. "Were you thinking of me, Callie?"

"I was. I was looking at my bucket list, wondering how you'd feel if I called you up and asked you to do something with me so that I can cross it off my list."

Mason's heart accelerated into a flat-out gallop and all the moisture in his mouth dried up. "As I recall, there were only two items on your list that you couldn't manage on your own. A one-night stand and phone sex. I'm happy to help with either, darlin'."

Very, very happy to help. He was a good guy that way.

Callie didn't reply and Mason could easily imagine her blushing, staring at the ceiling in mortification. The silence between them widened and Mason was about to back off, to crack a joke to break the tension, when Callie spoke again.

"If I can't even ask you for phone sex how can I actually do it?" Callie whispered.

Thank you, baby Jesus.

Mason closed his eyes, relief seeping out of every pore. He was already rock-hard at the suggestion and he wanted Callie wet and writhing as well.

"I'd love to have phone sex with you, Cal."

Callie's sigh of relief was audible. After a moment, she spoke again. "So, how does this work? Do I just say a whole bunch of sexy stuff?"

Mason was glad she couldn't see his grin. "Why don't you let me make love to you, Cal?"

"You can do that?" Callie asked, skeptically.

Damn straight he could. Mason released a low laugh. He'd start with the easy stuff. "What are you wearing?"

"Uh…um." Callie hesitated. "A short black transparent negligee?"

No, she wasn't. Mason suspected she was wearing something comfortable, something she wore every night. "I think you are wearing a long T-shirt and sleeping shorts, maybe just the shirt. Your hair is down, you have no makeup on and your eyes are that stunning shade I call horny blue."

"God." Callie released her first moan and Mason

felt like he'd won a million-dollar lotto ticket. He intended to have her moaning a lot longer. "For your information, Cal, I don't need to see you in negligees or heels. As soon as I see you, no matter what you are wearing, I go instantly hard."

"You…do?"

How could she not have noticed? Mason brushed his hand over his engorged dick, wishing it was Callie touching him. "Are you imagining me there with you? Wishing I was?"

"Yes. So much." Then Callie surprised him by continuing. "I'm thinking about kissing you, your tongue touching mine."

"I love your mouth, Cal." Mason slipped his palm under the band of his pants to take himself in hand. "I'm kissing my way down your neck, Cal, licking my way across your collarbone, sucking the creamy skin on your shoulder. You have such gorgeous skin."

Callie released a quick, sharp sigh and he heard a tiny gasp. Was she as turned on as he was? God, he wished he could see her. He considered suggesting they switch to a video call, but he couldn't risk spooking her so he pushed the idea aside.

"I'm thinking about my arms being around you, pulling you in. Your softness pressing against my hardness and trust me, Cal—" he brushed his thumb over this tip "—I'm hard everywhere."

"Are you touching yourself right now?" he asked.

"Um…no?"

Mason bit the inside of his lip to keep from laughing out loud. "Honey, how am I going to make you come if you don't touch yourself?"

Mason made a few more graphic suggestions and wondered how much longer he could last.

"God, Mace. This is so hot."

They hadn't even gotten to the good part yet. Mason clutched the sheets on his bed, not wanting to finish before she did. This was all about Callie.

Everything was about Callie.

This wasn't some random female he wanted to love and leave, this woman—older than him, requiring more effort than he normally was prepared to put in—was Callie Brogan. Wife, mother, widow, yes, but that wasn't how he saw her. He simply saw a woman comfortable in her own skin, someone who'd loved and lost and wore her scars proudly. Wise, funny, giving…not someone he could play with.

What the hell was she doing?

Despite her brave talk about not wanting a relationship, she wasn't the type who would give herself to any man without some sort of emotional connection.

He didn't do connections, emotional or otherwise. Keeping his boys' heads on straight was hard enough and he didn't want the responsibility of making another person happy.

His skills only extended to making a woman in his bedroom happy—after that they were on their own.

"Mace?"

"Yeah?"

"You stopped talking, I thought I lost you."

He closed his eyes. "Maybe we should stop this, Cal."

Callie released a low wail. "You have got to be kidding me! Why?"

"I can't give you what you want, honey."

"Right now, all I want from you is an orgasm," Callie retorted, her words covered in a layer of fierceness. "I swear, if you leave me hanging, I will disembowel you with a butter knife."

The corners of Mason's mouth lifted at her threat.

"Now, where were we?" Callie demanded. "Are you touching yourself, Mason? Do you wish your hand was mine?"

She had no damn idea how much.

DJ woke up slowly, her eyelids heavy as she fought the urge to snuggle down, to drift off again. It was still dark and she forced her eyes open, looked toward her window to judge the time. Did she still have an hour or three to snooze?

The drapes on her window were closed but she could see a bright sliver of light near the window frame. Why were her drapes closed? They had no neighbors on this side of the house so privacy wasn't a problem and she couldn't remember when last she'd pulled the drapes.

DJ tried to roll out of bed, but then the warmth of a male arm tightened around her and she tensed. Matt was hogging most of her big bed, his head on her pillow, his jaw rough with stubble. His spiky eyelashes lay against his cheek. His mouth, usually pulled into a stern line, looked relaxed and fuller in sleep.

Like her, Matt was naked and DJ was struck by how right it felt to wake up with this big man in her bed. The crisp hair on his chest tickled her nipple and her hip was half on his hard stomach. Under her cheek, she could feel the impressive bulge of his biceps, the smooth male skin.

Her knee rested on his hard-as-steel morning erection.

Somehow this felt more normal than waking up alone. Matt hogging the bed, holding her tight, made her feel secure, content, so very well loved.

Last night had been such fun, far more enjoyable than she ever thought possible. After tugging her around the rink and finally getting her to skate without falling for a few yards—she wasn't ever going to skate for fame or fortune—she and Matt joined the rest of the clan in the Frog Pond Café to warm up. Matt, with his dry sense of humor, had them cracking up with his observations about their fellow skaters. When Levi asked him about his work, he captured their attention by recounting some of his more interesting cases. DJ, who followed his career more closely than they did, immediately realized that he didn't talk about his biggest wins or the high-profile trials he was involved in. Possibly because those cases were filled with despair and tragedy.

It took a strong man to deal with what he did, DJ decided. He delved into a world few people had knowledge of. Political and war refugees, international criminals, the darker side of humanity. She understood his need to detach, to stay uninvolved. If he didn't, he wouldn't be able to do his job. Was his emotional detachment a habit? Was that why he wasn't interested in commitment?

DJ sighed. Why was she suddenly so curious? Why did she suddenly want to know the answers to these questions? They weren't going anywhere serious; they couldn't. In a few weeks, he'd be leaving her and Boston and she didn't know when she'd next see him. She never asked for the details of his life, because she couldn't afford to feel close to him, to create an emotional tie that would make her miss him more than she already did.

They didn't do ties, emotional or otherwise.

What they had was mutual respect and sex. Hot, crazy, wild sex.

Except that…

They hadn't.

They hadn't had sex last night, they'd made—dammit to hell and back—love. Sweet, sexy, soul-on-fire love.

It had been emotional and touching and, God, wonderful. It was fairy-tale sex. Sex like she wanted to have for the rest of her life. It was sex that walked hand in hand with early-morning snuggling, lighthearted arguments over whose turn it was to make coffee, pick up milk and buy takeout.

DJ tensed, annoyed with herself. It had been one night—*one night!*—and now she was picking out crockery and thinking about a life together? Had amazing sex finally melted her brain?

She and Matt didn't have any type of future except for maybe a stolen weekend here and there. They lived on different continents, in different time zones. They both had careers that demanded enormous amounts of time and energy. There was no way they could have anything more than the next few weeks and, possibly, some hookups in the New Year. That was who they were, what they did.

DJ looked at his closed eyes, his strong profile, and told herself not to be stupid. Besides, neither of them wanted anything more, really. Despite her promise to try and be part of the Brogan clan, she was never going to give another person the chance to hurt her again. Her parents had taught her that lesson well.

This was about sex, fun, a fantasy. Matt was a hookup, not a husband.

Eight

"Morning," Matt muttered, his eyes still closed but his thumb making patterns on the bare skin above her hip. "Question—how long have we been asleep? Where's my coffee? What time is it?"

DJ picked up his wrist, looked at his expensive timepiece and frowned. "Your watch has stopped."

Matt cranked open one eye. "My watch is one of the most iconic brands in the world, it doesn't *stop*."

"Well, it says that it's ten."

Matt lifted his arm, squinted at the steel-blue face and nodded. "That's because it is ten. In the morning." Matt resettled his arm across her waist, her breast in his hand, holding her close.

It took a moment for it to sink in that she was

late, very late. "Matthew! I should've been at work three hours ago!"

"Nuh-uh. Apart from the fact that it's Saturday, last night the twins gave you the day off. Remember?" His eyes remained closed but a satisfied smile crossed his face. "They obviously suspected we'd need some time to recover." He waited a beat. "They weren't wrong."

There wasn't anything she wanted more than to lie here with Matt—well, maybe a cup of coffee came close—but she had checks to issue, orders to sign. Contracts to negotiate. And if she was being honest, she really wanted to put some distance between her and all those unwelcome feelings Matt pulled to the surface with his display of trust and his tender treatment of her.

DJ felt like he'd pushed the sharp end of a crowbar into a crack in her soul and was slowly prying her open to reveal the chaotic mess she was inside. She could sleep with him, but it was essential that she stopped confiding in him.

He was her lover who was leaving, not her friend.

She needed coffee. And an additional ten IQ points.

DJ wiggled out from under his arm and sat on the side of the bed. Seeing Matt's long-sleeved shirt lying on the floor by her feet, she pulled it over her head before picking up her phone. She swiped the screen and saw that she had a few text messages on the group she and the twins used to communicate.

Maybe there was a problem at the shop; they wanted her to come in; they needed her.

Her hopeful assumptions were way off base. It's nine thirty, guess you got some last night. Darby's message was accompanied by a few high fives and a thumbs-up.

Shop is quiet. Don't want to see you here was Jules's contribution to the conversation.

Dammit. DJ looked over her shoulder to Matt, who was lying on his side, his head propped up on his hand. Jules felt her stomach flip over and heat rushed to that space between her legs. Sexy guy...

She pouted. "I'm not going to work. I've been banished."

Matt's mouth twitched with amusement. "If I didn't have a healthy ego, I'd feel insulted by your disappointed tone." DJ felt his hand skim her hair. It was another tender gesture so DJ stood up and walked over to the window, pulling the drapes aside. Cracking the window an inch, she sucked in freezing air before resting her head against the cold glass. She felt on edge and jittery, as if there were a hundred tabs open in her brain and none were loading properly. What was wrong with her?

"What's going on in your head, Dylan-Jane?"

She couldn't answer him—she'd revealed too much last night and she needed to put a whole lot of space between them and whatever the hell she was feeling. Because it was strange and unfamiliar and she didn't understand any of it. And not understanding scared her...

DJ heard movement behind her. Matt rolled out of bed, stood up and stretched, blissfully unconcerned about his nakedness. And why should he be? He had the muscled, hard body of an athlete and a face that stopped traffic. She admired his long legs— and his butt—as he disappeared into the bathroom. She lightly banged her forehead against her window. *Pull yourself together, Winston. You are acting like a fool...*

Her phone buzzed with an incoming message and this time it was from Callie. Next Christmas event: Christmas tree buying followed by cookie making at my house. Friday. Invite Matt.

Matt walked out of the bathroom, picked up a pair of boxers and slid into them. Pushing his hands through his hair, he arched an eyebrow. "Can I get some coffee?"

"Sure." DJ followed him down the spiral staircase and leaned her forearms on the granite counter as he made himself at home in her kitchen. Having him in her space—wearing only boxers and a spectacular case of bedhead—felt right. She could see them doing this next week, next month, next...

Stop! Distance, Winston. This is your life, not a rom-com.

DJ looked down at the phone in her hand and switched mental gears. "Callie has invited you to go Christmas tree shopping and to make cookies next Friday."

Matt took two mugs from a shelf and dug through her selection of coffee pods. He selected two dark espressos and popped one into the machine. While he waited, he leaned his hip against the counter and smiled. "Why do you make it sound like a root canal?"

"Close. Firstly, Christmas tree shopping with the twins and Callie can go on for hours as they search for the perfect tree. Since all Christmas trees look the same to me, it's torture. And I'm not the cookie-baking type."

"So drink wine and watch."

Matt handed her a cup of coffee, his expression serious. "Why do you hate Christmas so much, Dylan-Jane?"

It was a good opportunity to practice keeping her emotional distance so she trotted out her stock answer. "It's a rip-off. A commercial exercise we're suckered into."

"Cynical," Matt said, preparing his own coffee.

DJ sighed when the rich dark taste hit her tongue. "Truthful. Listen, I know you feel the same way since you're the guy who flew back to The Hague on Christmas day last year to work."

"My client was in trouble. I don't hate Christmas, I just don't have a lot of experience with it." Matt leaned back and crossed his feet. "When I was a kid, there wasn't money for Christmas presents.

Hell, there was barely any money for rent." He saw her puzzled look and explained. "My grandparents were richer than God, but they cut my dad off when he got into trouble with alcohol and drugs. When he dropped out of college for the third time, they washed their hands of him."

DJ knew Matt wouldn't appreciate sympathy so she just held his gaze and listened.

"I went to live with my grandparents—lots of money, lots of luxury—but they were atheists so Christmas came and went like any other day in their house. Then I went off to college and Christmas breaks were spent skiing or on the beach—either way I was partying. Baking cookies, ice skating and tree shopping never featured." Matt lifted his mug to his mouth and took a sip. "Sounds nice, though."

Memories, hot but sweet, rushed in. "My dad loved Christmas, far more than my mother. He took me skating, shopping, to see the tree-lighting ceremony on Boston Common. We built snowmen and decorated the house."

"But now you loathe the season. So what happened?"

Don't answer, don't answer...

"He left. A week before Christmas he walked out, leaving me with my mom." DJ winced, aghast that she'd let so much slip. She never spoke about her dad and she hated talking about her mother.

Matt didn't make any false sounds of sympathy

or utter any platitudes. "A week before Christmas? That's harsh. Are you still in contact?"

DJ felt the prickle of tears in her throat. "Nope. He dropped out of my life completely the following year. It was around the time he remarried and replaced me with his stepdaughter."

Matt stared down into his coffee mug before shaking his head. "I swear, I think the ability to bear a child should be heavily regulated and subjected to strict application rules."

"I think I want to apply, Matt."

Her words came out of nowhere and Matt looked as shocked as she felt. She bit her lip and closed her eyes, wondering who she was becoming. This new person tolerated Christmas, wanted to move emotionally closer to Matt and kept opening her mouth to allow odd statements to escape.

Original DJ wanted to kick DJ Version Two off the nearest tall building.

Surprise settled onto Matt's handsome face. "Uh… I'm not sure what response you are looking for."

"You don't have to give me one." DJ stared at the V in the base of his throat. She shook her head, suddenly needing to admit the truth to herself. Out loud. "I think I do want a baby, Matt. Sometime in the future, I want someone of my own to love, someone who can't leave me."

DJ stared down at her coffee, wondering how he'd react, what he'd say about that deeply personal revelation. She'd rather him not say anything at all than have him utter a cliché. She was so stepping out of the box they'd drawn around their relationship. This wasn't fun or superficial. This was raw and deep and scary, but it was real. And honest. Maybe she was a little tired of shallow, maybe she was braver than she thought and maybe it was time to look deeper, to be more.

Matt looked poleaxed at her unexpected revelation, and she knew he needed more time to process what she'd said, this new path she'd put herself on. She stood up and patted his shoulder. "Ignore me, I'm just tired, Matt. Christmas makes me emotional. Don't worry, this is just some temporary seasonal craziness. After some food and coffee, I'll be back to my normal, distant, cynical self."

The problem with that statement was that, for the first time in forever, she wasn't sure she was speaking the truth.

And, worse than that, she didn't think Matt believed her.

When DJ walked into the media room of the Brogan house a few days later, Darby looked up from her corner of the massive leather couch and smiled. When DJ reached the fireplace, she held out her hands to the blaze before picking up Darby's glass of red wine and taking a healthy sip.

"Hey! Get your own!" Darby protested.

DJ took another defiant sip before passing the glass back to Darby. "Where's Jules?"

"She and Noah flew to Cancún to see someone about a super yacht. He to design it, she to decorate it."

DJ turned her head to look out the tall windows and sighed at the freezing rain. Cancún sounded awesome. Jules and Noah had the right idea. DJ flopped down onto the seat next to Darby and rested her head on the back of the couch. She sighed and closed her eyes, fighting the urge to doze off. Long days at work and long nights with Matt were taking their toll.

Darby lifted her bare feet—her toes were rocking a bright orange polish—and placed them on DJ's thigh. DJ looked closer and saw that Darby's big toes sported a butterfly sticker. "Cute."

"Thanks." Darby held her glass against her cheekbone. DJ felt her friend's eyes on her and turned to look into her beloved face. Knowing that Darby was going to interrogate her about Matt, DJ jumped in first. "Any interesting projects on the horizon?"

Her tactic worked because excitement flashed in Darby's thunderstorm eyes. "I've seen the bid documents for the new art gallery the city wants built, the one close to the MFA? They've placed an open call for submissions for the design. They'll select the best ten concepts and those architects will be allowed to submit their designs for consideration." Darby frowned. "The only problem is that Judah Huntley is throwing his hat into the ring."

"Who?"

"Judah Huntley is one of the world's best architects, described as a tour de force, a visionary, ruthless in his quest for design perfection. And, as I've heard, he's submitting a concept design."

Ah, damn. DJ placed her hand over Darby's knee. "You're a wonderful architect, Darbs."

Darby pouted. "It isn't fair that a man can be that talented, that smart and that hot."

DJ's eyebrows flew up at Darby's comment. "Hot?"

Darby leaned forward and dug her phone out of her pocket, then her fingers danced across the screen. When she handed DJ the phone Darby looked down into the very sexy face of a dark-eyed man in his midthirties. "Holy cupcakes with sprinkles."

"I can show you a photo with his shirt off," Darby offered.

DJ held up her hand. "I don't think my heart can stand it." She waved her hand in front of her face. "Phew, *hot* is too mild a word. Gorgeous, sex-on-a-stick."

"Let's not forget brilliant and ridiculously talented." Darby released a sigh and placed her phone facedown on the arm of the chair.

A thought occurred to DJ. "Question—why do you have a photo of Judah Huntley with his shirt off?"

Darby couldn't meet DJ's eyes. "I happened to Google him and a picture of him on a beach in Cyprus popped up."

"Just popped up?" DJ asked, skeptical.

"He was there with his opera-singer girlfriend. She has a house there," Darby muttered. "He's hot but I've heard he's an arrogant alpha-hole. Talking about hot men, how is yours?"

Damn, DJ had opened that door and Darby strolled on through. "Matt?"

"You say that as if there are a dozen others. Is he joining you for the cookie-making marathon?"

DJ rolled her eyes. "He's actually looking forward to it." So was she. It sounded like it was going to be fun. She narrowed her eyes at her friend. "Did you sprinkle some of your magic I-love-Christmas dust on him? On us?"

"Maybe," Darby replied, looking smug. "So, what is happening between you and Matt? You're spending every night together."

DJ leaned across Darby, took her empty glass, poured some wine into it and took a sip. When Darby reached for it, DJ held it against her chest. "Mine. Especially if you are going to make me talk."

"Then talk."

DJ pulled her hair to one side and placed her hand on Darby's foot. How to explain this? "Matt's arrival in Boston has been a catalyst for me."

"How so?"

"Just being with him, in his company, shakes me up, makes me think. It's like he's handed me a pair of glasses and I see the world clearly."

"He's done all that?" Darby had the right to sound skeptical.

"Not directly. But a lot has happened since he arrived, and I've been forced to look at my life and my interactions with people with a more critical eye." DJ shook her head. "I'm suddenly not content to skate on the surface, Darby. It's not all fun and games anymore."

"Do you have feelings for him?" Darby asked carefully.

"I've always had feelings for him, I wouldn't have slept with him for so long if I didn't. If you are asking me if I'm falling deeper into something, then…"

DJ hesitated, not wanting to verbalize her thoughts. It all felt a bit too real.

"Then?" Darby prompted.

"My head tells me I shouldn't want a relationship. I know how emotionally dangerous they can be. He definitely doesn't want one."

"But you're in one, DJ," Darby pointed out. "You've been in each other's lives for a long time and while it might not be the most conventional relationship in the world, it's still a relationship."

DJ released a frustrated sigh. "I know. Relationships are risky."

"Sure, but risk is part of living, part of life. And sometimes—like for twenty-five years—people don't let you down."

DJ groaned. "You just had to take the shot, didn't you?"

"Yeah." Darby grinned. "The point is worth repeating…some people don't let you down, some people are in it for the long haul. Maybe Matt can be that person, *your* person."

DJ would love to believe that, but he wasn't. She knew he wasn't because he kept reminding her he was returning to The Hague—he'd utter seemingly offhand comments designed to remind her not to expect anything more than the fling, with a definite expiration date, they were currently enjoying.

Besides, she'd been protecting herself for so long, how could she be expected to throw caution to the wind and place her heart in someone else's hands?

DJ looked at the bottle of wine and sighed. "There's a little wine left in that bottle. I'm going to be a good person and rescue it."

Darby handed her the bottle. "You make me proud, every day."

Nine

Work had Matt holed up in the study of Lockwood House for two full days, staring at phone records, surveillance footage and reading reams of case notes on his human-trafficking case. He had to make the tough decision on whether the Europol investigators had enough evidence to prosecute. In Matt's opinion, the case was still light and he wanted more.

He only had one chance to nail those bastards to the wall and they couldn't take a chance on circumstantial evidence. They needed solid, stick-like-glue evidence, as he told the lead investigator.

He was not a popular guy at Europol HQ at the moment.

Needing air and a sense of normalcy, he left Lockwood House shortly before lunch and headed downtown, reluctantly admitting that he needed to touch base with DJ. They hadn't connected for the past forty-eight hours and he missed her.

Why?

For years and years, they'd shared only snippets of time and, while he thought about her occasionally, he'd never felt this primal urge to see her face. Missing her had nothing to do with sex and the way they burned up the sheets. This was about making a connection.

He was due to return to Europe after Christmas and he and DJ were supposed to go back to normal, to resume their see-you-when-I-see-you relationship. A year ago, jumping in and out of her life felt normal, sophisticated, modern. Now it...didn't.

He wanted to see more of DJ. He wanted to meet his daughter and he wanted Emily to meet his... What was DJ? His girlfriend, his partner, his significant other? What she wasn't was his on-and-off lover. He definitely wanted them to be more on than off, but how could he juggle his career, Emily and DJ? All while he was living across the world.

Not seeing DJ every day, having an eight-hour flight between them, was a hellish thought.

Matt shook his head, annoyed with himself. He shouldn't be obsessing. Was he using DJ as a way to distract himself because he'd yet to hear from Emily and was worried that he wouldn't? Or to avoid facing the fact that his grandfather's mind was rapidly deteriorating? Over this year, he'd realized he was losing his grandfather, had discovered a daughter he never knew he had and lost a child he'd never met—maybe his biological clock was ticking.

Matt found parking a block from Winston and Brogan's showroom and opened his car door to the frigid, snow-tinged winter air. Buttoning his coat, he stepped onto the sidewalk and frowned. Was having a family—having children, *more children*—something he was considering?

That wasn't a game he'd ever been interested in. He was the product of family dysfunction and he had no idea how to be a husband or a dad. He'd be as much of a dad to Emily as she'd let him be—accepting that she already had a dad and Matt was very late to the game—but more kids and a partner shouldn't be on his agenda.

Besides, even if he decided he wanted a wife, family, kids and a cat, when would he have the time? His work took up everything he had and then some. It had been hard enough trying to carve out time to be with DJ last Christmas. The coming year, with the trial looming, was going to be hell.

As much as he wanted to keep whatever this new thing was with DJ, realistically he didn't have it in him to make space for her in his life. There were too many obstacles—her life was in Boston, his was in The Hague. She couldn't move, neither could he. It was impossible.

So why was he even thinking about her in those terms?

Futile and impossible.

"Are you just going to stand there and hover?"

Matt jerked his head up to see Darby standing outside the showroom, stamping her feet. She looked chic and professional. "Hey." Matt pushed his hand through his hair as he walked up to her. "Where have you been in this horrible weather?"

"I went to a bid presentation for a new art gallery that I'd love to design."

"That sounds exciting," Matt replied, genuinely interested.

"Yeah but I don't have a hope of getting it." Darby pulled a face as Matt opened the door to Winston and Brogan and allowed her to precede him. "Judah Huntley was there and the board of governors was salivating at the thought of getting the amazing Huntley to design their new gallery."

Matt grinned. "I met him once, at a cocktail party at the US embassy in Amsterdam."

"Embassy party? Ooh la la," Darby teased.

"Trust me, embassy parties are as tedious as hell. Judah and I were equally bored and we ended up hitting some clubs in Leidseplein."

"Is that the Dutch word for the red-light district?" Darby's eyes were full of humor.

Matt grinned. "No, funny girl. Is Dylan-Jane in?"

"She was when I left. Are you still joining us for cookie-making night on Friday? We've moved the venue from Mom's house to the coffee shop. Mom needed more production space."

Inside the showroom. Matt hung his coat on the hook next to Darby's. "How many cookies do you guys eat?"

Darby led Matt up the stairs to the offices on the second floor. "They aren't all for us. We send a lot to women's shelters in the city," Darby said, stopping by her office door. "This is me. Go pull DJ from her spreadsheets and take her to lunch. Better, take her Christmas shopping. She knows what I want, I emailed her the list."

Matt laughed, shook his head and walked the few steps to DJ's office. Rapping on the frame of the open door, he watched as she took her time to lift her head, her eyes foggy with concentration. They cleared, she smiled and fireworks went off in his brain.

"Matt, hi. This is a nice surprise." DJ, dressed from head to toe in black, stood up, effortlessly elegant. Her long hair was pulled up into a wispy twist and her eyes were the rich color of bitter chocolate behind her black-framed, hot-as-hell glasses.

Hands off, Edwards. "I've come to take you for an early lunch. And Darby wants me to take you Christmas shopping."

"Okay."

Matt walked over to her and put his hand on her forehead, dramatically checking her temperature. "Are you feeling all right? I'm talking about Christmas shopping, with cheery music and crowds and commercialism."

DJ pushed his hand away. "I'm reconsidering my

stance on Christmas. So far this season hasn't been that bad."

"God, you *are* ill. Lie down, take off all your clothes and I'll check you for spots and injuries."

DJ laughed. "Funny."

DJ lifted her mouth to kiss him, then hesitated. To hell with that. Hooking his finger into the low waistband of her pants, he pulled her to him, holding her lovely face in his other hand and lowering his mouth to hers.

The first taste of her was a shock—there was a minor jolt of electricity to his heart and groin before he sighed and settled into the kiss. Slim arms encircled his neck and fingers pushed into his hair, danced across his jaw. Thoughts of trafficked girls and kids, gun runners and drug smugglers—and annoyed lead investigators—fled and there was only DJ…

Always DJ.

The thought rocked Matt and he pulled his mouth from hers, avoiding her puzzled look by holding her head against his chest. He could feel his fingers tingling and his heart pounding out a terrified beat. No, that couldn't be the way he was thinking. His off-the-chain thought was just a reaction to kissing her, to not seeing her for a day or two.

You normally don't see her for months and you've never had these thoughts before…

Shut the hell up, brain.

DJ wiggled out of his tight embrace and stepped away from him. "Everything okay?"

Matt kept his face blank and prepared to lie his ass off. He was only looking at his life and feeling like it was a distorted version of what he thought he wanted. Only when he put DJ into the picture, did the picture come into focus.

Really, Edwards? There was no way for them to have more than they currently did; they lived different lives on different continents. Besides, except for that one-off comment about having kids, DJ had never so much as hinted that she wanted more from him. He didn't have more! He was giving her all he could.

"Sure, why wouldn't it be?"

Matt walked over to the window and placed his hand against the cool glass. He felt off-center and weird, thoroughly disconcerted. How had DJ morphed from being the woman he wanted to occasionally spend time with, into the woman he wanted to spend *all* his time with?

Was it Boston? Christmas? A brain tumor?

DJ perched on the arm of her sofa and crossed her legs. "Actually, I was about to call you. Please feel free to say no but my mom has invited us to supper. She wants to meet the famous lawyer I'm dating."

Matt frowned. "Yeah, right." He scoffed. "I'm not famous."

"Apparently you have a bit of a rep for being a great lawyer. Strange but true."

Matt smiled at her gentle teasing.

"Anyway, Fenella wants to meet you and while

I'd rather get my eyes dug from my skull with a hot teaspoon, I can't say no. You can. Say no, Matt. I like you too much to subject you to Fenella Carew."

Matt picked up the conversational hand grenade Darby dropped at his feet. "Carew is your mother? The ex–attorney general of Massachusetts?"

Darby snapped her fingers and pointed her index finger at him. "Yeah. Lucky me."

Matt tipped his head to the side. "Judging by your underwhelming response, I assume she was a better lawyer than she was a mother."

"Much. One of my biggest fears is that I could, one day, be a mom like Fenella. Uninvolved, narcissistic, self-obsessed."

Matt just looked at her, his eyes steady on her face. He arched one eyebrow in a silent request for her to keep talking.

DJ threw her hands up into the air. "Why do I keep telling you stuff? Your eyes are like a truth drug! One look and I'm spilling my soul. It's very annoying," she complained.

Matt felt both proud and worried that this woman, the one who hated to talk, seemed to talk so easily to him.

"As a little girl, I loved pretty dresses, shoes, hair bands, anything that was pink and girlie, the more glitter the better. Every birthday and every Christmas all I wanted was makeup, plastic jewelry, tiaras and princess dresses. But she insisted I wear jeans, plain white shirts, ugly sneakers. Then she'd tell whoever would listen that I dressed like a boy, that she wished I'd act more like a girl. The next time I got ready to go out, I'd wear a dress and she'd tell me I looked dreadful and make me take it off." DJ folded her arms across her chest, her body language defensive. "My entire life was a constant stream of mixed messages."

"Babe." Not knowing what else to say, he hoped his one word would convey sympathy and sorrow and put a little warmth back into her eyes.

Matt reached out to take her hand, but she wouldn't meet his eyes, choosing instead to look out the window behind him. Her honesty made him wonder whether he'd be an uninterested dad like his father, or an autocrat like his grandfather. Neither, he decided, since he was never going to put himself in a place where he needed to raise a kid from scratch.

But he could ease some of DJ's fears now. "That's not you, DJ... She's not you. God, you are her exact opposite."

"I'm not," DJ protested. "Like her, I'm a perfectionist, uptight and anal. I overthink everything. My brain never shuts down."

"You're also honest. You told me about getting pregnant, told me about the miscarriage, you were open and forthright. You might not *like* to open up, but, when you do, you don't play games. You are nothing like your mother."

DJ started to argue but a squeeze of his fingers on her thigh kept her from speaking. "And instead of looking at Fenella as a role model, maybe you should start paying attention to your real mom and what she taught you."

DJ cocked her head, not understanding. One side of Matt's mouth lifted in a half smile. "DJ, Callie has been more your mom than anyone else. You've told me, more than once, that she was the one who bandaged your knees, gave you hugs, picked you up and dusted you off. You don't think you are a part of the Brogan family but you are the only person who thinks that. Callie worries about you as much as she worries about the twins and Levi, the Lockwood crew. Not a day goes by without her touching base with you, and she tells you every day that she loves you. She's your mom, DJ, by choice. And that sometimes means more."

God, he was her lover not her psychologist, her bed buddy not her life coach. DJ had lived on this planet quite successfully for nearly thirty years—she didn't need heartfelt advice from him. This wasn't what he did; this wasn't who they were.

Matt felt like he was standing on quicksand while his world rocked from side to side. Maybe he should book a plane ticket, fly to Europe and get a dose of reality. His grandfather was due to be moved into the assisted-living facility sometime between Christmas and the New Year. Matt could skip the festivities with the Brogans and return sometime before the New Year. If Emily was ready to meet him, they could do it after Christmas. That would give him some distance from DJ and, judging by that hearts-and-flowers speech, he needed some damn space.

Not that he was being insincere—he meant every word—but he didn't need her looking at him with stars in her eyes.

DJ stood on her toes and brushed her lips against his mouth in a tender kiss that rocked him on his emotional heels. He could do rough and wild, hot and fast, but emotion-soaked kisses were his down-fall. DJ followed up that bombshell kiss by brushing her thumb against his lower lip.

He watched, discombobulated, as she picked up her phone and tapped out a message. Seconds later his device beeped. "My mom's address, in case one of us runs late. She wants us there by seven. Don't say I didn't warn you."

Matt heard the faint buzz of his phone ringing in his pocket and pulled it out. With luck it would be his assistant or a colleague, someone who would bring him back down to planet Earth with a little legal-speak. He looked down at the screen and saw Emily's name.

Of course it was. Because, obviously, life didn't think he had enough on his plate right now. He shot a glance at DJ, realizing that he had yet to tell her about his daughter. Should he have told her? The old Matt, the one who just met up with DJ occasionally, wouldn't have bothered. But Boston Matt wanted to. He desperately wanted to ask her advice, to take her hand as he spoke to his daughter for the first time.

He was the person people leaned on, the one who steadied the ship, and yet here he was, looking to someone else—DJ—to do that for him.

No. That didn't work for him.

Matt pushed steel into his spine and turned his back to DJ as he answered his daughter's call.

"Emily? Hi, this is a surprise."

"Hi. I've been up all night thinking. I can't keep jerking you around, so if you want to meet, we can do that now."

Matt looked at DJ, who'd picked up her phone and was scrolling through it, but he knew she was listening to every word he uttered. He'd just invited her out for lunch and shopping, but he was going to bail on her. If he didn't meet Emily now, who knew when she'd find her nerve again?

"Yeah, okay, I can do that. Where are you?"

"I'll send you a GPS pin with the diner's coordinates. Just hurry, okay? I'm scared I'm going to bolt."

A cold hand squeezed his heart. "Please don't, Emily. I really want to see you." Matt looked at his watch. "I'm on my way. Ten minutes, okay?"

Matt turned to Dylan-Jane, not surprised to see her puzzled expression. He knew she was about to ask who Emily was, why he needed to run. He didn't have the time to answer, he just needed to get to his car so he could see his daughter.

He clamped his lips together, not trusting himself to speak.

To spill.

But, crap, he wanted to. He wanted to share this news, his worry and excitement, with DJ. Because the urge rocked him, Matt took a bunch of mental steps backward.

Emily and DJ were two very separate parts of his life. Emily was linked to him, by blood and responsibility, and she was a consequence of actions he'd taken a long time ago. DJ was his fun, a way to step out of his very busy life and relax. These two parts of his life didn't need to merge.

He hadn't promised DJ anything beyond good sex and some laughs.

Running scared, Edwards?

Damn straight he was and he was okay with that.

DJ grabbed his arm as he walked past her. "Matt, what's going on? Who is Emily?"

He jerked his arm away, fighting the urge to hold her, to let her hold him. He needed distance *now*. He needed to sever this connection, and fast, before he caved.

"I don't have the time to deal with your jealousy, Dylan-Jane."

Matt watched pain flare in her eyes as his words struck their target. And, yep, he felt his heart cramp. Well, it was no less than he deserved.

DJ's eyebrows flew upward. "What? Where did that come from?"

Matt felt overwhelmed, not an emotion he was accustomed to experiencing. He ran a hand over his face, wishing the floor would open up and let him slide on through. "I need to go, DJ. Emily isn't relevant to our relationship."

He'd resorted to lawyer-speak, a new low.

DJ nodded once, her eyes blank and her expression wooden. Her voice was cool when she asked her next question. "Do we even have a relationship, Matt?"

They were doing this *now*?

"Yeah, sure. What we have works for us because we don't make demands on each other. Not for time or information." He glanced at his watch, saw seconds ticking by and thought about Emily bolting. "I really do need to go."

DJ nodded once before making an exaggerated gesture toward her office door. "Then, please, don't let me hold you up."

Her voice was bland, but the part of him that wasn't terrified about meeting Emily and confused by the emotions churning inside him realized there was a note of anger in her voice.

"Goodbye, Matt."

That sounded like finality. Okay, maybe he'd overplayed his hand, but Emily was waiting. "I'll see you later, Dylan-Jane. If not at your place, then at your mother's."

"Yay," she muttered to his departing back and her words drifted over to him. "Misery loves company."

Ten

DJ lifted her fist to her mouth and stared at the door Matt slammed shut behind him.

What in the name of all things sweet and holy had just happened? One minute she'd felt like she was the center of his world, like he genuinely cared about her, and the next he was trotting out his we're-only-sleeping-together shtick.

One moment she'd been standing in his spotlight while he chased away the menacing shadows of her childhood. In that moment, it felt like they had one heart, a shared soul. Because words were inadequate, she'd kissed him, reached up to brush her mouth against his lips to try and convey how much she appreciated his insight.

Matt had always seen more of who she really was

than she was comfortable with. Maybe that was why she kept him at a distance, why she never allowed their conversations to go very deep. Because she knew that if she did, she could fall for him.

He was the one man she'd allowed to peer into the murky haze that made up her soul. But, because she was so damn scared of getting hurt, of letting any man see her tangled mess of insecurities, she'd tried to keep him at a distance, knowing she could slip into love.

As she was doing now.

Slipping? Was she already there? Probably?

Almost definitely…

Lately, once or twice she'd thought Matt might be feeling more. It was in the way he looked at her, touched her, the way his actions spoke so much louder than words. The way he listened to what she had to say.

She'd genuinely thought something was shifting between them but his words and actions after his strange phone call blew that notion to hell and back. Underneath her confusion, fury rumbled.

How dare he think she was jealous because she asked a simple question? She absolutely knew Matt wasn't talking to another lover. One, she and Matt had an agreement—if they were together then they were *together*. They didn't cheat. But it was obvious that Emily, whoever the hell she was, was important to him. DJ understood that Matt had a life apart from hers, but it wasn't a crime to ask him for a peek inside that world.

Really, it wasn't like she'd asked him to marry her next Tuesday.

What was the big deal?

She released a long, irritated stream of air before realizing that Matt rarely talked about his childhood or, God forbid, his feelings. DJ was the only one spilling her secrets and showing her soul. She'd talked about her father, his abandonment and how that had affected not only her views toward Christmas, but also toward men and relationships in general. She'd spoken about her mixed emotions over the loss of their baby and now, not twenty minutes ago, she'd told him all about Fenella.

Matt now *knew* her. She didn't know him.

DJ heard her door open and her heart lurched—she stupidly thought that Matt had returned, that he'd come back to apologize. But her hopes were dashed when Darby entered DJ's office, her expression concerned.

"Everything okay?" Darby asked. "I saw Matt rushing past like his pants were on fire."

DJ sank down on the arm of her sofa and shook her head. "I have no idea."

Darby frowned, closed the door behind her and sat on the coffee table in front of DJ. "What happened? He looked pretty relaxed when I spoke to him earlier."

DJ held her hands up. "I was talking to him about

Fenella—she invited us to supper tonight—and I was explaining that she was hell to live with, how I never knew which way to jump because she was so damn inconsistent—"

"Talking about your mom, another breakthrough," Darby murmured. "When you start talking about your dad, I'll know that your wall is about to tumble."

DJ dropped her eyes and Darby gasped. "You told Matt about your dad? God, DJ, you never speak about him, not even to us."

Yet another way DJ had refused to open up. "I'm sorry, Darby."

Darby waved away her words. "I'm just thrilled that you are speaking to *somebody* about him. Go, Matt!" She frowned when DJ shook her head. "Or not. Tell me what happened, sweetie."

"He got a phone call from a woman. He called her Emily."

"Oh, hell." Darby did the math and added up incorrectly.

"No, it wasn't that type of call," DJ protested. "Emily isn't a girlfriend." DJ held up her hand to silence Darby's protest. "She's *not*, Darby. Trust me on this."

"Okay," Darby said, doubt in her voice.

"I asked who she was and he nearly snapped my head off. He made it very clear that I had no right to question him, that we didn't have that type of relationship."

"The snot-shoveling piece of a rat's—"

DJ interrupted Darby's rapidly escalating tirade. "He's right, though, Darby. We're only bed buddies. Our relationship was based on fun and good food, wine and truly excellent sex. Talking was not part of the fantasy."

"But I'm sensing that's changed?"

"Yes. For me, at least. Him? Not so much."

"How has it changed?"

It was too late to back away now, to switch subjects or to halt this conversation. But why did she need to? Darby was her oldest friend and she trusted her implicitly. "Because he's the only guy I can imagine doing this with."

"Doing what, darling?" Darby softly asked.

Dammit, Darby was going to make DJ verbalize it because Darby knew that articulating these feelings meant they couldn't be easily dismissed or denied. Once DJ said it, it would be out there, a living, breathing, tangible thing.

They both jumped when Jules poked her head through the door, her eyes bright with curiosity. "What's going on?"

Darby waved her in. "DJ is about to tell me that she's in love with Matt," Darby said, her eyes not leaving DJ's face.

"I'm not, I don't think…" Yep, there she was, backtracking like mad. Ah, crap. DJ closed her eyes and jumped. "I'm in love with Matt, but I don't want to be. We've just had a huge fight, he won't talk to me and we're going to my mother's for dinner!"

"Call it off, DJ. You have enough to deal with without adding Furious Fenella to the mix."

DJ was about to agree with Darby, then she realized that, maybe, this was an opportunity not to be missed. If she pulled out all the stops—fantastic designer dress, do-me shoes, sexy hair and smoky eyes—she could show Matt what he was missing. Make him think about sticking around, trying to make something work between them.

DJ tipped her head and looked at her best friends. "I need your help."

They nodded, almost simultaneously.

"What do we need?" Darby asked. "A getaway van, a shovel, some rope?"

Jules rolled her eyes at her twin. "Seriously, you worry me. What do you need us to do, DJ?"

It warmed DJ to know these were friends who would move a body for her. But she needed something else today, something she'd enjoy less. "Come shopping with me."

DJ stood in her mother's expensively decorated white-on-white-on-whiter living room and clutched a glass of sparkling water to her chest.

As he always did, Jim, Fenella's closest confidant for the past fifteen years, offered DJ a glass of what she was sure would be an utterly delicious red. DJ wasn't brave enough to take the risk. She recognized

the upholstery fabric; it was shockingly expensive.
And the white carpet under their feet was just as
pricey. Red wine, white furniture and nerves were
a dangerous combination.

"I thought you said Matt was coming with you,"
Fenella said, obviously annoyed.

Nice to see you, too, Mom. "I'm sorry he couldn't
make it," DJ quietly murmured.

"Did he give you a reason?"

Actually, no, she hadn't spoken to him since he
walked out of her office hours before. She'd been too
proud to call him and when he failed to make an appearance at her door by seven, she pulled on her coat
and gloves and hat and walked the short distance to
Fenella's house. He had the address, he'd either rock
up or he wouldn't. It was out of her control.

DJ's solo appearance was greeted with as much
enthusiasm as an audit visit from the IRS. DJ looked
around the room as an awkward silence descended.
No tree, no decorations, not even a hint of Christmas anywhere. Funny that she'd never noticed her
mother's lack of Christmas spirit before.

The delicate chime of the doorbell catapulted
Fenella to her feet. She scuttled to the hallway to
yank open the front door. DJ folded her arms and
watched Matt step inside, his enigmatic eyes meeting hers over Fenella's blond head. His eyes widened as he took in her body-skimming black dress.
She felt his hot gaze like a caress, down her cleav-
age, over her hips, onto her exposed thighs. His eyes

widened when he noticed the fire-engine red works of art on her feet.

DJ half smiled as he had to wrench his gaze upward. Her outfit had put a house-sized dent in her bank account, but his gobsmacked reaction was worth every penny.

She was damned if she'd make it easy for him to walk away, and if he did, she'd wanted to make it hard for him to forget her.

DJ took a sip from her glass of water—she was a little surprised that he was here. Yes, he'd said he would be, but she'd expected him to use their fight as an excuse not to attend.

But then she remembered that this was a man who wasn't afraid of conflict: he took on sovereign governments, warlords and irascible judges for a living. He most certainly would be able to handle her narcissistic mother.

DJ saw Matt hand over a bottle of what she knew to be a phenomenally expensive champagne before he removed his designer coat. His dark gray suit was tailored, his shirt white, his tie the color of old charcoal. He looked urbane and successful and every inch the powerful lawyer he was reputed to be.

But as he stepped into the living room, DJ saw the strain on his face, the banked emotion in his eyes. Whatever happened at his impromptu lunch date had upset him and DJ cursed herself for caring. Why should she, since she was just his bed buddy?

DJ placed her glass of water on the mantel, watch-

ing as Matt shook hands with Jim and was handed
a glass of red. So, despite his tough day he wasn't
nervous and had no worries about Fenella's white
furniture and scathing tongue. Matt took a sip and
briefly closed his eyes before engaging with Fenella.

DJ lifted her chin and narrowed her eyes. He
might be able to ignore what happened between them
earlier, but she was still feeling raw and exposed and
very off balance. She was no longer the same person
she'd been a year ago. She didn't think she could pretend his lack of communication didn't matter. It *did*
matter to her. She wanted more, dammit.

She was terrified that she wanted *everything*.

She couldn't do this. It was too risky. She was
opening herself up to the possibility of too much
pain.

DJ pushed her fist into her sternum and ordered
herself to breathe. She'd been so very close to throwing caution to the wind and telling him she wanted
him, that she might love him. But what was the
point?

They could never have anything more than the
stolen weekends they'd had for the past seven years.
While lovely, those weekends were like light-as-air
chocolate mousse. Terrifically tasty but lacking
substance. After spending so much time with him
lately—all but living with him, sharing her body
with him—there was no way she could go back to
two-day weekends in hotel rooms.

Wanting more and never getting it would be slow

torture. It would slowly kill the little they had. It was only a matter of time before they split up. They were simply delaying the inevitable. Why not call it quits now? They'd had no contact for nearly a year before Matt came to Boston and they'd survived. They could just pretend the past little while was only slightly longer than a normal weekend and go their separate ways, no harm, no foul.

Okay, maybe a little harm and a little foul. But not nearly as much as there would be if she kept going with this until he finally decided she wasn't what he wanted, until he met the woman he couldn't live without.

She was, as her dad had taught her, easily replaceable.

She needed to leave, on her terms this time. She'd be in control. She'd be the one to walk away. She was never letting anyone leave her again.

"Dylan-Jane."

Matt's deep voice had her lifting her head because pride—the same pride that pulled her through years of living with Fenella—refused to show him that he was the one person she'd wanted to choose her.

It was over, it had to be.

The risk was too great, the reward—stolen weekends and nothing more—too small.

"Matt."

Matt bent his head to place a kiss on her cheek and DJ cursed herself because she so badly wanted to step into his arms, lay her head on his chest.

"Damn, you're mad at me."

Well, yeah. "Why are you here?" she asked him, keeping her voice low.

"There was no way I was sending you into battle without backup," Matt softly replied before stepping back.

Damn him for being sweet, and sensitive to how vulnerable she felt around Fenella. Just when DJ felt that she should push him away, he did or said something that made her desperate for him to stay.

"I can handle my mother."

"Why should you have to do it alone?"

Because you are leaving, and I have to? Because I've done it all my life?

DJ, seeing her mother approaching—Fenella could not bear to be left out of a conversation—swallowed her response.

"I'm so glad you're here, Matthew, albeit a little late. Let's go into the dining room. I don't want the pastry on my beef Wellington to get soggy."

Her beef Wellington? Fenella hadn't cooked anything more complicated than scrambled eggs in twenty or more years.

Fenella placed her hand in the crook of Matt's elbow and, ignoring DJ, led Matt away.

Situation normal.

Matt looked across Fenella's exquisitely decorated dinner table to meet DJ's eyes and his stomach tied itself in another knot.

Stop eyeing her like she's a pretty Christmas present you can't wait to unwrap, Edwards.

He took a sip of wine and wondered when this damn day would ever end. He'd had tough days before—in his line of work tough days were a given—but today ranked right up there. It had been a day of emotion, and emotion wasn't something he was accustomed to dealing with. He was very aware that he'd behaved badly toward DJ. Biting her head off when she asked about Emily was a dick move. And insinuating that she was jealous had been a double dick move. Not his finest moment.

The one thing he now knew was that his head and heart were at war. About his life, his career, Emily… Dylan-Jane.

His head and his heart were arguing about everything he most cared about.

Emily had been everything he'd suspected she'd be: smart, funny, confident. While his brain told him to stay aloof, to keep his distance, his heart—idiot organ that it was—flopped at Emily's feet. He liked her and, ten minutes after meeting her, liked that she was in his life. She was a part of him, someone he'd be connected to forever, a commitment he *welcomed…*

He was welcoming commitment into his life. Matt resisted the urge to look for a flying pig.

Maybe he was shaking free of the shackles of his past. Maybe he was, finally, acting like the adult he'd always thought himself to be. Maybe it was a combination of Emily, DJ and being back in Boston, but he felt freer, less constrained, able to look at his circumstances with clarity.

The one thing his heart and head agreed on was that he'd acted like a prize asshat earlier.

And a dishonest one at that.

It wasn't DJ's fault that he'd felt overwhelmed by the realization that she was far more than a casual bed buddy, that he didn't want whatever they had to end. Honestly, he wanted more but he didn't know how to make that work.

A good start, Matt decided, would be to apologize and tell DJ that Emily was the reason he'd come back to Boston.

Matt, feeling battered, released a long internal sigh. He hadn't felt so off-kilter since he was a child and a teenager, unsure of his place in either his parents' or grandparents' worlds. And that he hated feeling insecure was exactly why he never risked everything in a relationship. Since Gemma, the closest he'd come to love was liking Dylan-Jane.

But here he was on the knife edge of love. And it was a damn terrifying place to be. Because love hurt, dammit. It always had. It hurt when his parents chose their pursuit of pleasure—booze, drugs, partying—over his need for stability or a new winter coat or food. It hurt when he saw the frustration and resentment in his grandparents' eyes when their quiet, academic house was invaded by a sports-playing, smart-mouthed teenage boy, who ate more in a meal than they did in a week.

It hurt when he'd wanted so badly to be loved and had been forced to the periphery of their lives. That was why he'd fallen so hard for Gemma, Emily's birth mom. At seventeen, he'd dreamed of them marrying, creating a family, loving and being loved in return.

Her note telling him that she'd miscarried, that she was breaking up with him and moving away, had rocked him. From that day on, his relationships were only about the sex. He was comfortable with that, he knew how to handle it. He didn't know, as evidenced by today's screwup, how to deal with this churning cocktail of emotion that DJ whipped up.

She was—in the best, most exciting way possible—his biggest nightmare. She'd made him—as a grown, educated man—want to revisit those naive, foolish boy's dreams.

He could sit here and analyze this to death or he could do something, choose a course of action and stick to it. He'd start by telling DJ how he felt, see if she was, maybe, on the same page. He wanted to share his bubbling, nervous joy about Emily. But first he had to get through this damned dinner.

Fenella offered both him and Jim another serving of beef Wellington, but not DJ. Matt frowned. With her bland blond hair and faded blue eyes, Fenella—in her midfifties—was competing with her dark-haired beauty of a daughter. She knew she was fighting a losing battle, and that made her a little more pointed, a shade meaner. Every sentence she directed at DJ

was condescending, every time DJ spoke Fenella
interrupted. He'd been tempted to call her out, but
he knew DJ wouldn't appreciate his interference so
he'd kept his tongue between his teeth. He was convinced it was covered in bite marks.

But there was a point to this dinner and he wondered when they would get to it. After giving his
stock answers to oft-asked questions regarding his
more well-known trials, he felt a measure of relief
when Fenella stood up and asked Jim to help her
fetch the dessert, gaily waiving off their offer to
help.

As soon as they left the room, DJ lifted her eyes to
meet his. "Having fun?" she asked, her gaze frosty.

"No. It's as sucky as you suggested," Matt suc-
cinctly replied. "We need to talk."

DJ played with her heavy dessert spoon, tapping
it against the edge of a side plate. "Yes, all right. I
think it's time we cleared the air."

Good, great… *Calm the hell down, heart.* He
could do this. Firstly, he'd apologize and explain
about Emily, about why he'd been so off his game
earlier. After he got that done—hopefully without
making a totally mess of it—he'd tell her that he had
feelings for her. Feelings that were new to him, feelings she'd hopefully reciprocate. They would agree
to spend Christmas together, take some time to work
out how they could see each other more often, how
they could talk every day. They'd make it work.

Every problem had a solution.

He wasn't convinced. Matt felt like his internal organs were caught in a vise. What he wouldn't give to be staring down a war-crimes defendant or a three-panel lineup of the world's most educated judges. *That* he could handle.

Matt looked into Dylan-Jane's eyes and felt his panic fade. Anchoring himself, he fell into the depth of emotion he saw there. She looked scared yet defiant, emotional but holding it together. He was about to tell her that everything would be okay—he would make damn sure of it—when the door opened and Fenella and Jim returned, each carrying two tiny ramekins. Her eyes darted from DJ's face to his, but beneath her smile lay the heart of a barracuda.

Fenella placed a small dish in front of DJ, then walked around the table and reached over Matt's shoulder to place his dessert on the table in front of him. There was no need for her to push her breast into his shoulder, for her mouth to pass so close to his ear. Matt ignored her and kept his eyes on DJ, hoping she wouldn't notice her mother's inappropriateness. DJ, thank God, had her head down as she tapped the bowl of her spoon against the hard topping of her dessert. She didn't notice Fenella's fingers dancing across the back of his neck.

Matt gave Fenella a cut-it-out look and she responded with a sexy smile. Fenella slipped back into her chair and, judging by the speculative look she and Jim exchanged, Matt knew she was about to drop the conversational equivalent of a hand grenade.

"I'm sure you've forgotten, Dylan-Jane, because you seldom remember what is important to me, that I am the chairperson of Boston Women." DJ looked up, her eyes wary. She swallowed her mouthful of dessert and carefully replaced her spoon on the side plate next to her.

Fenella looked at Matt. He knew she was waiting for him to look impressed, but he'd never heard of the group before. He lifted his hands. "Sorry, should that mean something to me?"

"We are an exceptionally influential group of like-minded women—intellectuals, professionals, business people who gather to discuss topics of mutual interest."

Sounded like hell, Matt thought.

"We are a think tank, a discussion group, but we do one charity event a year and that's our Christmas ball. It's an extremely elite gathering of the movers and shakers of Boston and I intend to, formally, announce my senate run at this year's ball."

"Congratulations," Matt murmured. What else was there to say? And why did he feel like she'd yet to pull the pin on that grenade?

"We only issue two hundred invitations and guests are carefully debated. Invitations are coveted. Very influential people will be present."

She'd said that already. God, he needed this to be done so he could talk to DJ. She was important, this crap about a ball wasn't.

"Every year we have a keynote speaker and this year we've nominated you."

What? Matt jerked up, his eyes flying to Fenella's face. "Me? Why?"

"You're smart, successful and interesting. You're young and good-looking and have had interesting experiences, and successes, in international law and human rights. People remember your grandfather and he is a legal legend. People would be interested in what you have to say and the contacts you'll make will be out of this world."

Except that he didn't work in Boston, he worked in The Hague. Boston contacts wouldn't do squat for him there. He looked at DJ and lifted his eyebrows. "You going?"

"No." DJ's eyes turned flat and cold. "I'm not nearly important enough to warrant an invitation."

"Darling, I just don't want you feeling like a fish out of water." Fenella's patronizing smile made Matt slam his teeth together.

"She has an MBA, Fenella, I think she can hold her own." Matt pushed the words out between his teeth.

Jim jumped into the conversation. "For you, there is no downside, Matt. It would raise your profile and, let's be honest, there will be a host of legal talent in the room. Your surname is gold and there's nothing wrong with being associated with one of the brightest legal minds of this generation," Jim said, his tone jovial. "Having successful, influential people around

Fenella makes an impression. Knowing that you endorse her might sway some of the on-the-fence donors, people who are worried about the conservative slant she's taking."

Oh, hell no. "But I'm not endorsing her."

Jim ignored Matt's statement. "We certainly don't expect you to shout it from the rooftops. In fact, any overt political support at this event is frowned upon. People prefer more upbeat, motivational speeches, but the members of the committee were persuaded that you were the best choice. People will know Fenella has a personal connection to you. She will take the credit for you speaking."

They made it sound like he was just going to hop on through the hoops they were holding up. Like crap. He decided to test them. "I presume that my invitation will include Dylan-Jane as my plus one?"

Fenella's mouth tightened. "I'm afraid not. There simply isn't space at the main table and the tickets were snapped up months ago."

Yep, an F minus for lack of effort. Matt picked up his napkin and tossed it on the table. "Not interested." He looked at DJ and sighed at her colorless face. This was the crap she'd dealt with all her life? He'd endured two hours and he was at his limit. "Wrong answer, Fenella."

Fenella smiled. "Matthew, Dylan-Jane knows where she is most comfortable and it's not in a ballroom with two hundred people far more successful than she will ever be."

Matt shook his head, stunned at Fenella's lack of maternal instinct or common decency. Matt was on the edge of losing his temper. He rarely let loose, but when he did, international judges, opposing counsel, clerks and his staff knew it was best to run for cover. Taking a deep breath, he counted to ten, then to twenty, but the words still bubbled like acid on his tongue.

He wasn't going to be able to hold back—the urge to defend his woman was too strong, too primal. But before he could speak, DJ pushed her chair away from the table and flung down her linen napkin, her eyes angry and defiant.

She placed her hands flat on the table and glared at Fenella. "Take your ticket and shove it, Fenella. I would rather go to hell on a melting ice cube than endure hours in a stuffy ballroom listening to you put me down. In fact, I'm never putting myself through that again."

Fenella laid her hand on her heart and sighed. "Stop being dramatic, darling. I've had a nice night and you're spoiling it."

"You've spoiled many years of my life so I'm pretty sure you'll cope. The only reason you bothered to invite me to dinner tonight was to get Matt here. Putting up with me was the price you had to pay because my lover is a successful, well-respected human-rights lawyer."

God, she was magnificent—dark eyes flashing, cheeks flushed, breasts heaving.

Fenella and Jim exchanged a long look and Matt thought, just for a minute, that Fenella might lie and reassure DJ that Fenella had wanted to see her daughter, that she enjoyed DJ's company.

Then Fenella shrugged and leaned back in her chair. "My highest priority is my career and my political ambitions."

And there it was, in black and white. What a princess.

"No, Fenella, your highest priority is yourself. It always has been, everything has always been about you."

"Do stop with the dramatics, Dylan-Jane."

Matt saw DJ's jaw tense and knew she was grinding her teeth together. "You refuse to see me, Fenella, for the person I am. I am a partner in one of the fastest growing design businesses in the city. I'm financially fluid and respected by the people I work with."

"The Brogan twins?" Fenella scoffed. "Please! Callie Brogan used to have some influence but since Ray passed away, she's not as socially active as she used to be. She's less than useless. Noah Lockwood has the cachet of the family name, but he keeps a low profile, so what good is he to me?"

"It's not all about you!" DJ shouted.

Fenella smiled, her eyes as cold as an Arctic wind. "Of course it is, because it sure as hell isn't about you."

Right, this had gone on long enough. He had to

leave now because soon there wouldn't be enough bail money in the world.

But Dylan-Jane wasn't done. He saw the smallest of smiles cross her face, then her shoulders dropped and she looked at her mother with contempt. "Thank you, Fenella."

Fenella frowned at her odd response. "For what?"

"For saying that. Now I can walk away, completely guilt-free."

"This really is getting tedious."

DJ nodded. "I absolutely agree. And after I walk out that door, I'm done. I'm done with you and your narcissistic personality and your weird desire to put me down. I have no value to you and you sure as hell have no value to me. So let's break up, huh, Mom? What do you say?"

Fenella's mouth dropped open and Matt was completely sure this had to be the first time Fenella was ever caught by surprise.

"Now, let's not be too hasty…" Jim said.

DJ's cold glare stopped Jim in his tracks. "This is long overdue, Jim. I should've had the guts to do this years ago. Goodbye, Fenella. I'd say I'd vote for you, but that's a lie."

Then his woman—this amazing, brave, confident woman—picked up a full, open bottle of red wine. Walking away, DJ defiantly tipped the bottle upside down and a stream of red hit the carpet. He followed the river to the hallway, amazed and thrilled, by how quickly the stain spread. It was petty, admittedly, but fun.

After all, even he could tell the place definitely needed a splash of color.

Eleven

As DJ walked out of Fenella's house, she knew she would never be back. Never again would she worry about saying the wrong thing, waiting for the caustic bite of a sharp tongue, the stinging slap of a derogatory comment. She would never again wish that she was a better daughter, someone her mother could love. Her mom couldn't or wouldn't love her and DJ was done waiting for Fenella's approval.

DJ was done. Period.

As she hurried back to her apartment above Levi's house, she heard Matt's footsteps behind her. When they reached the Brogan house, his hand on her elbow stopped her in her tracks. DJ turned to face him, conscious of the icy air on her cheeks, the heat of their breaths creating a cloud between them.

Matt...

In the twinkling lights from the surrounding houses, she realized that she was done wishing with him, too.

She needed to face reality and, for the first time, DJ felt strong enough to do that. Her father had replaced her, her mom didn't even like her and, to Matt, she was a way to pass time. She couldn't blame him for that. They'd both used each other. It had been done with respect and gentleness; they'd both taken what they needed before going back to their respective lives.

The problem was that she now wanted more.

Deep inside, she'd always wanted to feel like she was the center of someone's world, to be someone's first choice. Matt couldn't give her that, but DJ knew she couldn't settle for less. It was time to be her own champion.

DJ looked around, shook her head at the pretty houses, the decorated lawns. It was Christmas, the time of the year when everything momentous happened. Her father leaving her, getting pregnant with Matt's baby, walking away from Fenella...saying goodbye to Matt. For good.

DJ scowled at the elaborate, oversize wreath Darby had hung on the front door.

"Matt." DJ jammed her hands into the pockets of her coat. Standing in the freezing cold was not the best place to have a breakup chat, but, on the plus side, the frigid temperature would keep their conversation short. "Look, I—"

Matt held up his hand and DJ stopped speaking. She had no idea how to verbalize what she was thinking anyway. She'd never excelled at talking...

"I need to explain about Emily."

"Matt, it's not important."

"It *is* important. I owe you an apology, but before I get to that, I need to explain that Emily is my biological daughter."

What?

DJ just stared at him, her mouth slack with surprise.

"I was seventeen when I had a relationship with her mom. Gemma told me she miscarried, then she moved away and I didn't know she carried the baby to term and gave it up for adoption. Emily contacted me earlier this year and we started corresponding. Part of the reason I came to Boston was to meet her, but she got cold feet and asked for some time. Today she called me and invited me to lunch right then. I *had* to go."

DJ took a moment to process his words, to make sense of what he was saying. Then anger, regret and resentment churned inside her. "You've known about your daughter all this time and you couldn't tell me? Instead you insinuated that I might be jealous?"

Matt pushed an agitated hand through his hair. And looked embarrassed. "Look, you've got every right to be mad, but before you blow me off, which

I'm pretty sure you're about to do, I need to tell you that I'm—"

DJ held up a hand. She couldn't move off this topic, not just yet. "Hold on a sec, Matt."

DJ stamped her feet and hunched her shoulders. It was cold, sure, but this frigid iciness invading her body was a pain she'd never experienced before. It had nothing to do with the falling temperatures. "I need to get this straight. You come back to Boston and insist that I tell you what's worrying me. I tell you that I miscarried your baby. I tell you about my father leaving me and adopting his mistress's child. But I don't stop there, I also tell you about my narcissistic mother, who doesn't like me at all. I bared my soul to you, something I never, ever do and *you couldn't even tell me you have a daughter*?"

Oh, God, he really didn't see her as anything more than a bed buddy. She wasn't even his friend.

DJ shook her head. She hadn't felt this miserable since she'd watched her dad walk away that night two decades ago. What was it about Christmas and its need to kick her emotional ass?

"Dylan-Jane—"

"Don't you dare!" DJ said, nearly yelling. "Don't you dare utter some inane platitude, telling me you care about me, that you're sorry!"

"I am sorry. Very sorry," Matt murmured. "Let's go inside. We'll make coffee, have a rational conversation. DJ, we can fix this—*I* can fix it—if you'll just hear me out."

Matt reached for her hand, but DJ stepped back. She didn't need his comfort and she sure as hell didn't need his pity.

Sucking in her last reserves of energy, she took a step back, then another. Tossing her hair, she forced away her tears, needing to get this over with. "I'm calling it, Matt. We're done. We were wrong to try and mix what we had with our real lives. It got complicated, so let's…uncomplicate this."

Shock skittered across his face. *"What?"*

"Maybe it's time we both tried someone different, something different. I'm your go-to girl and I want to be someone's *everything*. You're the guy who can't give that to me."

Matt frowned at her, looking annoyed. "You're now making my decisions for me?"

DJ lifted her chin. "Matt, you couldn't even tell me about your past, that you once got a girl pregnant. My miscarriage was the perfect segue into that conversation, something like…'I can't believe this is happening to me again.' If you couldn't tell me that, after what I went through, how can I assume you will tell me anything personal, let alone how you feel about me?"

DJ threw up her hands in exasperation. "I love it how everybody thinks I have the problem communicating when you're a hundred times worse. At least I tried, Matt."

DJ saw a million emotions in his eyes, but because he didn't try to explain what was running through his mind, she had no idea what he was thinking. Yeah, it was way past time to stop flogging this almost-dead horse. It was far kinder just to put it down.

Despite not being able to imagine a world without Matt in it, DJ summoned her courage. "'Bye, Matt. I hope you'll be gracious enough to give me some space while you remain in Boston. And, merry Christmas."

"You don't believe in Christmas."

"Funny, I was beginning to."

DJ hurried into the yard and ran up the steps to her apartment before her tears started.

"DJ—" Matt called.

She'd never heard her name spoken with such regret and she wanted to go back to him, to soothe his pain away, but then the knot at the end of DJ's frayed rope snapped. One sob escaped, then another, and before she could release a third, she slipped into her apartment, closed the door behind her and sank to the floor.

Curled up into a ball, she finally let herself cry.

Mason heard the strident ring of his doorbell, wondering who was leaning on it at 10:20 p.m. on an icy winter's night. Walking from his study into the hall, he glanced up the stairs, thinking one of his boys would bound down to open the door. Only a teenager would be stupid enough to be out when the windchill took the temperature below zero.

No one charged down the stairs and the doorbell chimed again.

Annoyed, he yanked open the door and the small bundle on his doorstep whipped around. "Callie?"

He checked again... Yep, it was definitely Callie, red-nosed and looking nervous. "What are you doing here?"

"Are your boys here?"

"Upstairs," Mason replied, thoroughly disconcerted. "Is everything okay? Come inside."

Callie tipped back her head and shook her head. "I can't, not if your boys are here."

Damn, he was freezing and really, his boys wouldn't care if he had a guest. Seeing the obstinate tilt to Callie's chin, he sighed. "I can sneak you into my study, they'd never know."

"If and when I agree to date you, Mason James, it will be openly and honestly. I'm far too old to be sneaking around."

Okay, that sounded promising, but it still didn't explain why she was on his doorstep. "Can you put on a coat and shoes and come out here for a bit?" Callie asked.

It was ridiculously cold, but Mason was starting to realize there wasn't much he wouldn't do for her. Mason shoved his feet into the pair of boots he left by the door and grabbed his coat and scarf. Pulling on both, he closed the door behind him.

He stamped his feet and sent her a quizzical look. "What's this about, Cal?"

In the dim light of his porch, he saw determination sweep aside nervousness and then she pushed her hands into his coat and put them on his chest. Standing on her tiptoes, her mouth brushed his with the sweetest, hottest kiss he could remember.

She pulled back to whisper against his lips. "I thought about phoning you but I didn't want that, I wanted to be in your arms, I wanted to kiss you. Is that okay?" Callie asked, holding on to his coat to keep her balance.

Let me give that some thought... Yes.

Oh, hell, *yes.*

"Kiss away," he muttered, aiming for insouciant but hitting breathless. Now, there was a feeling he'd never, ever cop to. He allowed her to control the kiss, closed his eyes when her lips moved over his, kept his hands lightly on her hips as she gently sucked on his lower lip. He wanted to pull her in, take her, possess her, but this was a major move on her part and he didn't want to scare her off.

After minutes of sweet torture, he couldn't take any more. "Open your mouth to me, Cal, I want to taste you."

Her lips opened, her tongue darted out to meet his and he was lost. Groaning, he swept his hand under her coat to grab her butt, yanking her into him so she could feel how aroused he was, how much he wanted her. Forgetting his vow to take this slowly, to let her set the pace, he devoured her mouth, his tongue sliding against hers, dueling with her for control of their kiss.

Callie wanted this—*him*—as much as he did.

The thought slammed into him and he reacted, taking the kiss from lusty to fierce. God, he needed her, naked in his bed. Now, tonight, up against the wall, immediately.

He wrenched his mouth off hers, his lips exploring her fine jaw, sucking on the skin below her ear. "Let me come home with you, Cal. This is killing me."

"Mason."

Hearing the need in her voice, he yanked his head back to look at her. She was so close to saying yes, he could see it in her eyes, in the way she said his name.

"Say yes, Cal. Please. I'm begging here."

Callie opened her mouth to speak, only to be interrupted by the annoying ring of her phone.

Mason let rip with a long stream of curse words as Callie fumbled for her phone. She stabbed the screen with a shaking finger and he heard sex in her voice when she offered a breathy hello.

Mason, not giving up, ran his thumb over her lower lip and back again. He wanted those lips on various parts of his body and he'd been so close to getting it.

"Yeah, yeah, I'm there. Give me ten minutes."

Dammit. Whatever was said had killed the passion and he knew the moment had passed. Seriously, was the universe conspiring to keep him from having her, knowing every inch of her?

"I'm so sorry, I've got to go."

Mason watched her walk down his path to her low-slung sports car, his heart thundering and his dick straining against the buttons of his jeans. "Callie?"

"Yes?" She turned and Mason saw that her nervousness was back. She expected him to castigate her, to complain about her being a tease. She rubbed her forehead and he noticed her trembling bottom lip. She looked from him to her car and back again. "I have to go, DJ needs me."

She'd drop everything for one of her kids. As frustrated as he was, he had to respect that. But she could spare him a minute to hear what he had to say.

"We can't go on like this much longer. It's time to fish or cut bait. In or out."

"Mason…"

He ordered his heart to ignore the pleading look in her big eyes. "We *have* to move forward, Cal. I'm not asking for anything more than a night, two, as many as works for us. I need you, naked, in my bed and in my arms."

"You're pushing me, Mason."

Yeah, well, someone had to.

But he wanted her fully on board with where they were going and what they were doing, so he forced a cheeky smile onto his face. "I sent Santa my letter. You are all I want for Christmas. So when he calls you to make arrangements, don't be uncooperative."

A quick, appreciative smile took his breath away. "I'll see you tomorrow at your place."

For a moment he thought she was agreeing to sex, then he remembered that her clan was coming over to the café to make a million cookies. Super.

Callie lifted her hand and slid into her car. After a small wave, she pulled away, but it was a long, long time before he went back inside to his warm house.

DJ was lying against Darby's chest, her legs across Jules's lap. Callie sat on the coffee table facing them, shoving tissues into DJ's shaking hand. She couldn't remember when last she'd cried this much.

"I think I'm dehydrated," she whimpered, her voice rough from sobbing.

"You can't be dehydrated, DJ, you've had three glasses of wine." Darby lifted her hand to pat the side of DJ's head.

"Then I'm drunk," DJ decided.

"Much more likely," Callie briskly replied.

Leaning forward, she wiped a tear from DJ's cheek and sent her a sympathetic smile. Callie had been DJ's second call when she'd picked herself up off the floor. The first had been to Darby, and within ten minutes all three women were in DJ's sitting room, doling out sympathy and wine in equal measure.

When you sent out an SOS this was what friends—no, *family*—did. No questions or qualifications; they just dropped what they were doing and ran. DJ looked at Jules, who'd obviously tumbled out of Noah's bed. She wore one of his sweatshirts and ratty yoga pants, and had shoved her feet into a pair of UGG boots. Darby wore men's pajamas, oversize. Callie? Callie looked as beautiful as ever, but why did she have what looked to be razor burn on her chin?

And God, that reminded DJ of how Matt would rub his stubble over her cheekbone, down her neck. She'd never feel that again. She'd never be held in his strong embrace, or curl her arms around his hard waist, or slide her hands down his thighs.

Oh, God, what had she done?

"You do realize you are not only mourning Matt, you are also grieving the death of your relationship with Fenella and your dad leaving you," Callie calmly stated. "As well as the loss of your baby."

"My dad left a long time ago, my mom is as mean as a rabid snake and I wasn't ready for a baby, so I'm pretty sure I'm only crying about Matt," DJ said, feeling exhausted.

"Now you're just being stubborn, Dylan-Jane," Callie said. "You've had a constant hope that things would get better between you and Fenella. You've always dreamed your dad would come waltzing in to claim you, to apologize for leaving all those years ago. Of course you're mourning your baby because, deep down in that place you won't look at, you've always wanted a baby. That's why you are also crying over Matt. He's the one person you could see yourself making a family with. They are all connected, darling."

"Matt was only ever just a bit of fun," DJ protested.

If she told herself that often enough maybe she'd start believing her lie.

"You conned yourself into thinking that was all he was," Callie told her, her voice insistent. "DJ, do you really think you would've kept seeing him for all these years if you weren't crazy about the man? If it was just about the sex, you would've stopped seeing him years ago."

"I don't know, Mom, he is pretty hot," Darby commented. "I might've stayed around just for the sex."

Callie ignored her. "You will be okay, Dylan-Jane, with or without Matt in your life."

DJ looked at the only real mom she'd ever known, desperately wanting to believe her. "How do you know?"

"Because when Ray died, I thought I did, too. For years and years, I wondered why I was here, what the point was." She heard her daughters gasp and held up her hand to keep them from interrupting. "I wasn't myself for a long time. I just…functioned."

"I know I can't compare my pain to yours, Cal. You were married to Ray for more than thirty years…but losing Matt still hurts."

"Yeah, love does hurt. But just remember, if you can feel pain so deeply, you can love just as deeply. That's the yin and yang, my darling."

"I want Matt to love me," DJ finally admitted. "But he doesn't."

Callie took DJ's hands, snotty tissues and all, in hers. "But, honey, that doesn't mean he's the only man you can love. While it's romantic to think there is one man out there to share your life with, it's practical to remember that relationships sometimes don't work out, people die, hearts break. It's a part of life, part of being human. But I'm begging you, DJ, don't retreat. Don't let this pain stop you from being open to finding and receiving love again."

DJ couldn't imagine being held, kissed and touched by anyone other than Matt. On an intellectual level, Callie's words made sense, but everything in DJ rebelled at the thought.

Yet she knew Callie meant well so DJ tried to smile. "Maybe by next Christmas I might be ready to throw myself back into the dating game."

"Oh, it'll be long before that. Maybe by then, Jules will have provided me with a grandbaby I can spoil."

"Can I get married first?" Jules demanded, shaking her head in exasperation. "And why don't you harangue our brother like this?"

"Oh, I hassle him about his love life and I also spend many minutes on my knees praying that God will send him a girl who will lead him in a merry dance. Since Tanna broke off the engagement—"

"She all but left him at the altar, Mom!" Jules interjected, frowning.

Callie waved away her correction. "Anyway, your

brother is far too used to getting his own way with women."

The twins bumped fists. "Amen, sister."

"As for you, Darby Brogan, I have a wonderful feeling you are going to get exactly what you want... and more importantly, what you need."

DJ could feel Darby's smile. "I hope that means a baby, Mom."

"You'll get what you most need, Darby Brynn Brogan," Callie reiterated, before slapping her thighs and standing up. She bent over and clasped DJ's face in her hands before placing her lips against DJ's forehead in a long kiss. "I love you, baby girl. I could rip Fenella's throat out for hurting you, and if I could, I would kick your father's butt to hell and back. But you will be okay, DJ."

"You didn't threaten Matt, Mom," Darby pointed out.

Callie held DJ's eyes. "No, I didn't. I think that boy will surprise us yet." She gestured to the pile of tissues and the empty bottle of wine. "I'm going back to bed."

DJ thanked Callie and they watched her walk out, gently closing the door behind her.

Jules tipped her head to the side. "Was that stubble burn on her jaw? Do you think Hot Coffee Guy put it there?"

Darby scowled. "That's not the point, Jules. What I want to know is why I am the only one in this room not seeing any action."

Twelve

They'd both caught feelings. Like damn amateurs.

DJ was right. And it pissed him off to admit that.

He'd waltzed into her life expecting her to tell him everything. He'd demanded it because he was the guy who asked the questions, who got answers, who made assumptions and created strategy around what people said. He never allowed his perceptions to cloud a situation; he stayed emotionally uninvolved.

He hadn't realized that he'd been treating DJ like a client. Even though he knew he was falling for her, knew he was feeling more for her than he should, he'd still kept his distance, choosing to listen rather than engage. He'd treated her like…

God, he'd treated her like his parents and grand-parents had treated him.

Looking from the outside in, he'd done just enough to remain in control but not enough to be a full—or even half—partner in the situation. DJ did what she did and he just reacted.

Matt felt rocked by the realization. He'd genuinely thought he was better than that.

Now Matt looked at the small wooden table and watched Emily's mouth moving, automatically tucking her words into the boxes where they belonged. Her plans for the New Year, her college roommate, her best friend. Listening to her, but still reeling from the night before, Matt desperately hoped his pounding head, tight throat and fuzzy thinking were a result of a sleepless night and not because his heart was curled up in a corner whimpering.

He'd thought he was tougher than that.

"So I'm thinking of dropping out of college to go smoke pot in a commune in Peru."

Matt heard Emily's words and knew they were a test, to see if he was listening. She'd have to do better than that; he could listen to three conversations and read a book at the same time.

"Over my dead body," Matt muttered, ordering another cup of coffee.

"So you were listening but you definitely weren't paying attention," Emily said. "I have to say, I'm a bit annoyed that I'm not the entire focus of your universe right now since I've only recently dropped into your life."

Matt wanted to feel bad about not giving her the

attention she deserved, but he was feeling so crappy already that he didn't have the energy. "Sorry, I have a lot on my mind."

"Like?" Emily demanded.

Matt started to change the subject and realized that was something he always did when he didn't want to answer a personal question. But Emily, like DJ, wasn't a random person. Emily was his daughter. And if he wanted her in his life, he needed to let her in.

"I've been seeing someone on a casual basis for many years and she just called it quits."

"Ah. Couldn't have been that casual, then."

Matt frowned at her. "What do you mean?"

"If you are upset and stressed, which you so are, you obviously have deeper feelings for her than you realized. Does she have feelings for you?"

"I think she does."

"And the problem is?"

The problem is that I'm scared. Soul-deep terrified.

He knew what it was like to live with someone and not be loved, to be a part of someone's life and not be valued. Love, as he knew it, wasn't a guarantee for a happy-ever-after. But relationships didn't come with guarantees.

Maybe it was better that he hadn't laid his heart on the line, hadn't expressed all his hopes for what he and DJ could be. At least, this way, he still had his pride.

But his pride wouldn't keep him warm at night, make him laugh or feed his soul.

Dammit.

"It doesn't matter, I'm going to let her go and you and I can be a family," Matt said, leaning back so the waitress could put a cup of coffee in front of him.

"A part-time daughter you'd see once or twice a year? That's your definition of a family? No wonder your girlfriend dumped you." Emily rested her forearms on the table. She wrinkled her nose before nailing him with a look. "Do you want a family, Matt?"

"I have you," Matt carefully replied.

"That wasn't what I asked."

Sure, he wanted a family. He wanted someone to come home to, kids who ran into his arms, a wife who kissed him awake and blew his mind, and other body parts, at night. But that was a fantasy... He'd had two families and both had been terrible. With his work schedule, he was pretty sure he would be terrible at it, too.

"I work a lot, Emily. My life is crazy."

"So, uncrazy it. You choose how much you work. Last time I heard, there wasn't a law that said you needed to put in such long hours."

Ah, the folly of youth, so black-and-white. "It's not that simple, Emily."

"No, you're just making it complicated. Do you know why you want to call me your family, Matt?"

"Because you, actually, are?"

"Okay, biologically, yes, but I'm not, not really.

This may hurt and I'm sorry if it does, but I already have a dad. He's the one I ride motorbikes with, who sends me stupid dad jokes, who once drove eight hours to take me to a dance competition. He's the one I would turn to if my life fell apart, he's the one who's going to walk me down the aisle. You will be my friend, I hope, but he's my *dad*."

Matt felt like a red-hot blade was being shoved into his heart. For the second time in twenty-four hours.

"But you want all that, I can see it in your eyes. You want a daughter you can take to dance class, a son you can take to soccer. A wife who loves you. You want a family."

Matt couldn't speak. If he did, he might finally lose it.

"There's this woman out there who might want that, too, with you. Don't you think you owe it to her, and yourself, to see if a family is something you can make together?"

"We both have issues…" It was pathetic but it was all he had.

"God, you old people are so lame. Everybody has issues, Matt. Deal with it."

He was getting schooled by an eighteen-year-old. That being said, he was still proud of the strong, sassy, in-your-face woman she was. "Your parents did a wonderful job with you, Emily."

She grinned. "I know."

Matt looked at his watch. "Do you want to meet her?"

"The person you nearly let slip through your fingers? Sure."

"It might mean making Christmas cookies."

"My mom is the Christmas-cookie queen. I smoke at making cookies. And, this way, I can make sure you don't chicken out at the last minute."

Yeah, she was smart. And too damn cocky.

Exactly like he'd been at her age.

DJ was trying her level best to get into the spirit of Christmas, she really was.

Mason had rearranged the café's tables so they were all in a long row and they had a sort of cookie production line going. Levi, Eli and Ben, under Callie's supervision, mixed ingredients. Mason and Noah rolled out the dough. Jules pressed out shapes and Darby put them onto cookie sheets, which Callie put in the industrial oven. Because DJ had arrived late, she was tasked with making various colors of frosting and putting them into bags so they could decorate the cookies when they cooled.

The twins, with their keen eyes for color, felt the need to supervise DJ's every step, and the making of the red icing had taken ten minutes longer than it should have before they were both happy with the color. Instead of resisting, DJ quietly followed their orders, thinking that it didn't matter whether they ended up with a fire-engine red or something darker. Red was red and her heart was still broken...

DJ looked down the table and caught Noah looking at Jules. DJ watched passion cloud her friend's eyes as Jules stared back at her man. Unable to watch, DJ moved on to Callie only to see her watching Mason, confusion and desire and fear on her face.

DJ's heart, that stupid, hopeful organ, still wanted what Jules had, what Callie and Ray had enjoyed for thirty and more years—a partner, somebody who made her life complete. A family.

Callie was right when she'd said that DJ needed more than what she'd been prepared to settle for. After being alone for a very long time, she'd thought being alone was safe, that she could be content with having a shallow relationship. But when Matt came into her Boston-based life everything changed. It suddenly made sense. He filled her world with laughter and fun and heat and really exceptional sex.

But Matt didn't see her as someone he could trust, someone he could lean on. She needed him to view her as an equal partner, as a friend and confidant as well as a lover. His silence told her, in actions louder than words, that she was, and always would be, just his bed buddy...

DJ picked up a bottle of green food coloring and tipped the bottle slowly so that a drop, then another, hit the white frosting. The first drop looked black and then, as it spread, it lightened into the brilliant green of Matt's eyes. In seeming slow motion, DJ saw her arm sweep the bowl off the table, watched as it hit the slate floor and shattered, green-tinged frosting exploding like a sugar bomb.

DJ looked down at the mess she'd made and burst into tears. It was all too much. Christmas and her dad and her mom and Matt and the emerald green frosting and the broken bowl and the ruined cookies and...

God, she *hated* Christmas.

DJ felt warm arms around her, a hand pulling her head to a chest and someone tugging a spatula from her fist. Sobbing harder, she pressed her wet face into a warm, masculine neck.

"Shh, DJ, don't cry," Matt murmured.

He was here? Even so, she honestly didn't think she'd ever be able to stop.

"I need to clean up. I made a mess."

"Mason's handling that."

Standing on her tiptoes, DJ looped her arms around Matt's neck and told herself she should let go. Walking away from him again was going to be harder than before. Hanging onto him like a wet limpet wasn't something she should be doing. She hung anyway.

DJ thought she felt Matt's lips in her hair, but then he was talking to Callie and Mason and his words didn't make sense. Then she heard a voice behind her, one she didn't recognize, but she couldn't find the energy to care. She was so tired...

"C'mon, DJ."

Holding her tight against him, Matt walked her across the room. At the front door, he lifted her coat from the hook. He carefully dressed her, pushing one arm into a sleeve, then the other, then buttoned her up before tightening the belt. Through her tears, DJ noticed Matt's brow was furrowed, his deep eyes worried. As Matt pulled open the door, DJ swiped the balls of her hands across her eyes, hoping to wipe away some of her tears.

Another batch just took their place.

On the sidewalk, Matt took her hand and walked her across the road to his car, yanking open the passenger door and guiding her inside. Matt slammed his door shut, started the car and fiddled with the heater before leaning back in his seat, his eyes finally connecting with hers.

When he made no effort to drive away or to speak, DJ gestured to the wheel. "Where are we going?"

"Nowhere. We have cookies to make and I want you to meet someone."

She was over anything to do with Christmas and she really wasn't up to meeting anyone new. This wasn't her finest moment.

"In case you didn't notice, this isn't a good time for me," she said, trying for sarcastic but hitting miserable instead.

Matt gripped the steering wheel with one hand and DJ noticed that his hand had lost all color. When she turned her eyes to him she noticed that his face was ashen, too. "And that's on me. I'm sorry, DJ."

"I'd like to tell you it's okay that you can't give me what I want—what I *need*—but I'm not there yet. That's why you have to keep your distance."

"Except that I don't want to."

DJ frowned. "I don't understand."

"I don't want to keep my distance. I don't want to be without you."

Oh, God, if this was a joke or a prank, she'd kill him, she really would. And if he made some stupid suggestion that fell short of what she needed, she'd maim him. And she'd make sure it hurt.

Before she could formulate a sentence, Matt picked up her icing-splattered hand and kissed her fingertips. The corners of his mouth kicked up. "Sweet. Literally."

"Matthew." His name on her lips was a plea for an explanation. Or to let her go.

Matt lifted her hands to his lips, held her knuckles against his mouth and closed his eyes. When he opened them again, DJ—for the first time—saw all the way down to his soul.

"I want more, Dylan-Jane. I want *everything*."

DJ stared at him, terrified that he was telling her what she most wanted to hear. And she was equally scared this entire encounter was a figment of her imagination. DJ pulled back, still half expecting him to open the door and walk away into the snow.

"Please don't say that if you don't mean it," DJ whispered. "Please don't tell me that if you intend to walk out of my life again."

Fury flashed in his eyes. "Why do you think I would do that, DJ?"

DJ turned her head to look out the windshield. "Just before my dad walked out of my life, he told me he loved me, that he'd always love me, but I never saw him again," she whispered.

"I swear to God..." Matt said, anger coating every word. DJ saw him push his frustration and fury away, and when his fingers slid around her neck and his thumb stroked her jaw, his expression was tender. "There's only you, DJ, there's only been you for the past seven years. I'm not walking away, Dylan-Jane, and every time I leave you, I *will* come back. That is my solemn promise."

She wanted to believe him, she did, but she felt like she was standing on a bridge with only a thin rope to stop her from slamming onto the sharp rocks below. If that rope broke...

"I want to be with you, Dylan-Jane, because you are the only person that makes sense. It's Christmas and, while you don't believe it, it is the season of miracles. You are *my* miracle, you've got to know that. I want to marry you and have babies with you and sleep with you and fight with you and, God, I want to love your delicious body for the rest of my life. I want you in my life, only you."

Matt waited a beat before speaking again. "Forever you. Be my Christmas miracle, DJ."

Then Matt spoke the words she most needed to

hear. "I love you, Dylan-Jane. To me you are, and always will be, irreplaceable."

More tears slid down her face, but DJ didn't care. She let her body expel the last of her fear, her distrust. Holding Matt's face in her hands, she wept. Matt, because he knew her so well, just waited until her tears slowed.

"Are you sure?" DJ asked, her words rasping from the tears still clogging her throat.

Matt half smiled. "About loving you? Yes. About never leaving you? Yes. About being irreplaceable? Damn straight."

DJ felt a smile start to bloom on her lips. She shook her head, trying to think clearly. Matt loved her! They had a future! She was emotionally safe!

"I don't know what to say," she admitted, turning her mouth to place a kiss on his palm.

The pad of Matt's thumb rolled over her bottom lip. "Then let me talk. We're going to get married, DJ, at some point, preferably as soon as possible. I haven't yet worked out how we'll manage two careers on separate continents, but I will—*we will*. And we will spend the bulk of our time together, that's not up for negotiation. This not seeing each other for weeks and months is BS and it's over...we *will* find another solution that works for both of us. It might mean splitting our time between two homes, but I don't care where we live as long as we are together."

A sunburst of happiness dried the rest of her tears and DJ opened her mouth to agree, but Matt shook his head and spoke over her. "I don't know how good I am going to be at being a husband or a dad, I didn't have great role models when it comes to either, but I swear I'll learn, DJ. I'll never cheat on you and you'll be my first priority, I promise."

She couldn't demand that of him; he had a daughter and she should come first. Putting their kids first was what good parents did. "You have Emily, Matt. I understand that she needs to come first."

"Emily has her dad, DJ, and a family she adores. I'm okay with that. But I want my own family, with you. I want to do better, be better at love and responsibility and raising kids than our parents were. You want to come along on that ride with me?"

There was so much hope and vulnerability in his voice. DJ slowly nodded as she held his intense gaze. "In time, I want another baby with you, Matt, maybe two. But before then, I want us to learn to lean on each other. I want to be your light when your work is dark, your rock when your ground feels shaky. It's going to be hard sometimes because life is hard, but if we put each other, and our kids, first we'll be okay. If we hold on tight to each other, we can love our way through anything."

Matt rested his forehead on hers, his breath sweet on her lips. "I love you, Dylan-Jane."

The sweetest words ever said. "I love you back, Matt."

"Want to marry me?"

God, *yes*. "More than anything," DJ whispered.

Matt's lips finally met hers and DJ's mouth curved under his. "Brace yourself, Matt, but I think I'm changing my mind about Christmas being the worst time of year."

Matt's low laugh drifted over her. She was the luckiest woman in the world because she was going to hear that laugh for the rest of her life. Not only that, but she also got to kiss this man, love this man, until she died.

DJ pulled back and looked at Matt. She really wanted to tell him how she was feeling, how happy he'd made her, how fulfilled she suddenly felt, but those damn words wouldn't come.

Matt nodded and smiled. "I know, baby. It's almost overwhelming, isn't it?"

DJ nodded. "I feel bigger, greater, like I'm about to burst out of my skin, like I am three sizes too big for this car. Like nothing is ever going to be the same ever again."

Then Matt kissed her and he felt both new and familiar, exciting and reassuring. He kissed her slowly, gently, his mouth telling her that she was loved, that she would never be alone again. That she would always, always have him standing next to her.

He was absolutely her Christmas miracle.

Then his tongue slipped between her open lips and passion rolled in, hot and demanding. Matt groaned into her mouth and his kiss turned possessive as he branded her as his. DJ didn't mind—it was, after all, the truth.

She was his and forever would be.

DJ wasn't sure how long they kissed, but when they heard the sharp rap on the window, her coat was off, Matt's hand was inside her bra and his erection was rock-hard under her hand. Thank God, the windows were solidly misted over. Matt cursed as he pulled away and when DJ thought they looked marginally presentable, she cracked the window an inch.

The three witches stood outside, smirks on their faces. "Well?"

DJ darted a look at Matt, who was leaning back in his seat, looking amused. He arched an eyebrow, silently telling her to answer Darby's demand.

"Well what?" DJ asked, trying to look innocent.

"I swear I'm going to kill you," Darby muttered. "Are you back together?"

DJ nodded. "Yes. In a way."

Darby made the sound of a momma wolf protecting her cub. Pushing a finger through the crack in the window, one gray eye glared at Matt. "I swear, Edwards, if you think you are going to get away with not making some commitment to her, I will chop you up with a chain saw."

Matt raised an eyebrow and smiled at DJ. "She's warming up to me, I'm sure of it."

DJ chuckled. "Want to be a bridesmaid, Darby?"

"If you think I am going to let you go back to that half-assed relationship you had, well, you can just forg—" Darby faltered. She frowned. "What did you just ask me? Are you getting married? When? Seriously? Mom, Jules, they are getting hitched! Will you please get out of this damn car?"

DJ laughed, glanced down at Matt's pants, saw he was on his way to being decent and grinned at him. "We need to go back inside. Sorry, but they'll hound us until we tell them everything."

Matt's finger ran down her jawline. "I know they are part of the package, sweetheart, and I wouldn't have it any other way. And yes, we do need to go inside. I'd like you to meet Emily."

DJ jerked back in shock. "Your daughter is in there and you left her alone with strangers?"

Matt shrugged. "She's a big girl and you needed me." Matt opened his door and a snowflake drifted into the car. But before leaving the car, he sent her a look that melted her. "I love you so goddamn much, Dylan-Jane. Never doubt that, okay?"

Now, there was a statement she could wrap her head around.

Epilogue

Mason stepped into the entryway of Callie's home and picked up a glass of champagne from the tray on the hall table. He was late because he'd spent Christmas Eve with Emmet and Teag and, thanks to the snow, his ex had been a half hour late to pick up their boys. It was now close to midnight, but the party was in full swing and there were a lot more people here than he'd expected.

In fact, the house was heaving with couples in ball gowns and tuxedos. Mason ran a hand down the lapel of his own tux, briefly wondering when last he'd worn it. Three years ago? Five?

Did that matter? All that mattered was that he was here, at the first Christmas Eve party Callie had thrown since before her husband's death. Mason sipped his champagne, wished it was whiskey and tried to spot his quarry, which was impossible given the fact that he couldn't look past the broad backs of Levi Brogan and the three Lockwood men.

God, he was frustrated. He hadn't been alone with Callie since that hot kiss on his porch ten days ago. Time was up. He wanted her. They would be damn good together. But she had to decide to fight for him, too.

Mason looked around and his attention was caught by the opposite wall, which was filled with family photographs. Wanting to ignore them, but knowing he couldn't, he sauntered over. His eye was immediately drawn to a photograph of a dark-haired man sitting on a wall, his head thrown back with laughter. Callie's Ray, Mason surmised. Levi looked like him, Darby had his nose and chin, Jules his eyes.

Intelligence and good humor radiated from him and Mason, whose ego was fairly healthy, felt intimidated. How the hell was he supposed to compete with Ray Brogan? While Mason was rich enough, he wasn't the billionaire Brogan had been. Neither was he as sociable—tattooed math geeks didn't tend to be—nor was he, his mouth twisted, as good-looking.

Jesus, what the hell was he doing here?

Mason was about to step back when a feminine hand slid into the crook of his arm and a subtle perfume hit his nose. He knew it wasn't Callie because his heart rate didn't accelerate. He slowly turned to see Darby standing next to him, her gaze on her father's face.

"You would've liked him, you know."

The hell of it was that he probably would have.

"And he would've liked you," Darby added. "He would've liked the fact that you don't take any nonsense from my mom. He didn't, either."

Mason didn't know whether to defend Callie or not, so he changed the subject. "Quite a crowd."

Darby grinned. "Yeah, Mom was wild about how Fenella treated DJ and decided to teach her a lesson. She knew a lot of people who'd bought tickets to Fenella's function tonight would rather attend one of the Brogans' Christmas Eve parties so she called them all up and invited them over to help her celebrate both Jules's and DJ's engagements. Fenella is going to have at least a third fewer people than she expected."

Mason had to smile. His woman wasn't someone to be messed with. He looked over to where DJ and Matt stood on the edge of the dance floor, supposedly dancing but really just swaying to the beat. Their gazes were locked on each other and anybody looking at them could see their love…and their desire to get naked as soon as possible.

Darby nudged Mason and he turned back to look down into her lovely face, a face that would look a lot like Callie's in twenty years. "You look at Mom like that."

Ah, God, what was he supposed to say to that?

The switch to another subject had worked for him before, so he tried it again. "Have DJ and Matt worked out their living arrangements?"

Darby smiled, amused. "They are still working it out but they will. They love each other too much to live apart. Are you in love with my mother?"

Mason almost dropped his glass in surprise. "Uh…"

"You are, aren't you?" Darby persisted.

Of course he wasn't! He wanted to sleep with her, that was all. He opened his mouth to explain, but how could he tell the grown-up daughter of the woman he lusted over that this was all about sex?

Can't do it…

"Whether I am or not has very little to do with you." Mason managed to push the words between his teeth.

"Fair point," Darby conceded. She looked at the photo of her dad and when her eyes met Mason's, hers reflected sadness in their silvery depths. "I love—loved—him. He was the best person in my life and he adored my mom. And she adored him."

Yeah, he'd worked that out. It was time to go.

Darby held his arm in a death grip. "This hurts like hell to admit, but I never saw her look at him the way she looks at you."

Whoa! Every muscle in Mason's body tensed as he waited for her next words, but pride wouldn't let him ask her to elaborate. After a minute—a millennium—Darby spoke again. "Maybe she and my dad sparked off each other when they were young, but the two of you? God, one look and boom! It's disconcerting, I have to tell you."

She should see it from his point of view.

"You do something for her, Mason, and whatever you are doing scares her. She's resisting. Keep doing it, though, because you've made my mom enjoy life again. For that I will always be grateful."

He felt he should explain. "Darby, listen, it's not like that. I'm not going to be your mom's happy-ever-after. That's not what's happening here. I get that you are concerned about her, but please don't start thinking that I'm her knight in shining armor. Because that would be crap."

Darby laughed. "Mason, my mom is a strong woman, we *all* are. We come from a long line of strong women and the last thing we need is a knight, in armor or otherwise. Brogan women slay our own dragons."

With that parting shot Darby drifted back to the crowd. Mason stepped away from the bank of photographs and glanced around, determined to find his quarry.

As if on command, the crowd parted and there she stood, looking glorious in a green fitted dress and sky-high heels, her blond hair tousled and her blue eyes dominating her face. She was talking to a man in his sixties who, judging by the look on his face, was working out the best way to get her into bed.

Hell, no. The only person she was going to bed with was Mason and it was time she got used to the idea.

He walked across the room, his eyes on her face, waiting for her to notice him. Her shoulders tensed, her back arched and her head spun around, blue eyes connecting with his. He debated whether he should go to her, whether she wanted to advertise their connection. Callie surprised him when she beckoned him over. When he reached her side, she lifted her fingers to touch his jaw. Her heels allowed her to brush her lips across his, giving him a longer than polite kiss.

Finally, his brain kicked into gear and he gripped the slim hand lying against his heart.

"What the hell are you doing?" he whispered, noticing that her eyes were dancing with amusement.

Under the amusement was flat-out lust. For him. He went rock-hard instantly so he turned his back to the room.

"A little show-and-tell," Callie said, taking another taste of his mouth.

Both hands were on his chest now and Mason knew the room was watching—the band had stopped playing.

Mason frowned. Who was this woman and what had she done with uptight Callie Brogan?

Callie looped her arms around his neck and ran her fingers through his hair. "I'm kissing you to show everyone here that you are here with me and I'm about to tell you exactly what I want for Christmas."

He couldn't pull his gaze away from her face. "What do you want for Christmas, Cal?"

"There were two things on my bucket list you said you could help me with…" Callie said, her cheeks now tinged with pink.

He forced himself to remember her list. One was phone sex and the other… Holy, holy crap. "You want a one-night stand? With me?"

Callie's nod nearly stopped his heart.

"Just one night of pleasure with no expectations, no strings. No demands. Can you give me that, Mason?"

It was the only thing he'd asked from Santa, the only item left on his Christmas list. This was what he wanted…*all* he wanted.

So this was turning out to be the best Christmas ever in the history of Christmases.

Then, as he fell into Callie's startlingly blue gaze, the thought occurred to him that, maybe, one night might not be enough.

* * * * *

*Can Mason and Callie have the one-night
stand they both think they want...
or will they find they need more?*

*And what will happen when Darby's world is
upended by a baby and a sexy architect who
doesn't want children...?*

Don't miss Darby's story,
The Rival's Heir,
available December 2018!

COMING NEXT MONTH FROM

HARLEQUIN® Desire

Available November 6, 2018

#2623 WANT ME, COWBOY

Copper Ridge • by Maisey Yates

When Isaiah Grayson places an ad for a convenient wife, no one compares to his assistant, Poppy Sinclair. Clearly the ideal candidate was there all along—and after only one kiss he wants her without question. Can he convince her to say yes without love?

#2624 MILLION DOLLAR BABY

Texas Cattleman's Club: Bachelor Auction

by Janice Maynard

When heiress Brooke Goodman rebels, her wild one-night stand turns out to be her coworker at the Texas Cattleman's Club! How will she resist him? Especially when the sexy Texan agrees to a temporary marriage so she can get her inheritance, *and* she learns she's expecting his child...

#2625 THE SECOND CHANCE

Alaskan Oil Barons • by Catherine Mann

The only thing Charles Mikkelson III has ever lost was his marriage to Shana. But when an accident erases the last five years of her life, it's a second chance to make things right. He wants her back—in his life, in his bed. Will their reunion last when her memory returns?

#2626 A TEXAN FOR CHRISTMAS

Billionaires and Babies • by Jules Bennett

Playboy Beau Elliot has come home to Pebblebrook Ranch for the holidays to prove he's a changed man. But before he can reconcile with his family, he discovers his illegitimate baby...and the walking fantasy of his live-in nanny. Will temptation turn him into a family man...or lead to his ruin?

#2627 SUBSTITUTE SEDUCTION

Sweet Tea and Scandal • by Cat Schield

Amateur sleuth: event planner London McCaffrey. Objective: take down an evil businessman. Task: seduce the man's brother, Harrison Crosby, to find the family's weaknesses. Rules: do not fall for him, no matter how darkly sexy he may be. He'll hate her when he learns the truth...

#2628 A CHRISTMAS TEMPTATION

The Eden Empire • by Karen Booth

Real estate tycoon Jake Wheeler needs this deal. But the one sister who doesn't want to sell is the same woman he had an affair with years ago... right before he broke her heart. Will she give him a second chance...in the boardroom *and* the bedroom?

YOU CAN FIND MORE INFORMATION ON UPCOMING HARLEQUIN® TITLES, FREE EXCERPTS AND MORE AT WWW.HARLEQUIN.COM.

HDCNM1018

She was going to be interviewing Isaiah's potential wife.

The man she had been in love with since she was a
teenage idiot, and was still in love with now that she was
an idiot in her late twenties.

There were a whole host of reasons she'd never, ever
let on about her feelings for him.

She loved her job. She loved Isaiah's family, who were
the closest thing she had to a family of her own.

She was also living in the small town of Copper Ridge,
Oregon, which was a bit strange for a girl from Seattle,
but she did like it. It had a different pace. But that meant
there was less opportunity for a social life. There were
fewer people to interact with. By default she, and the
other folks in town, ended up spending a lot of their free
time with the people they worked with every day. There
was nothing wrong with that. But it was just…

Mostly there wasn't enough of a break from Isaiah on
any given day.

But then, she also didn't enforce one. Didn't take one. She supposed she couldn't really blame the small-town location when the likely culprit of the entire situation was her.

"Place whatever ad you need to," he said, his tone abrupt. "When you meet the right woman, you'll know."

"I'll know," she echoed lamely.

"Yes. Nobody knows me better than you do, Poppy. I have faith that you'll pick the right wife for me."

With those awful words still ringing in the room, Isaiah left her there, sitting at her desk, feeling numb.

The fact of the matter was, she probably could pick him a perfect wife. Someone who would facilitate his life, and give him space when he needed it. Someone who was beautiful and fabulous in bed.

Yes, she knew exactly what Isaiah Grayson would think made a woman the perfect wife for him.

The sad thing was, Poppy didn't possess very many of those qualities herself.

And what she so desperately wanted was for Isaiah's perfect wife to be her.

But dreams were for other women. They always had been. Which meant some other woman was going to end up with Poppy's dream.

While she played matchmaker to the whole affair.

Don't miss what happens when Isaiah decides it's Poppy *who should be his convenient wife in*
Want Me, Cowboy *by* USA TODAY *bestselling author Maisey Yates, part of her Copper Ridge series!*

Available November 2018 wherever Harlequin® Desire books and ebooks are sold.

www.Harlequin.com

Want to give in to temptation with
steamy tales of irresistible desire?

Check out **Harlequin® Presents®,
Harlequin® Desire** and
Harlequin® Kimani™ Romance books!

New books available every month!

CONNECT WITH US AT:

Facebook.com/groups/HarlequinConnection

 Facebook.com/HarlequinBooks

 Twitter.com/HarlequinBooks

 Instagram.com/HarlequinBooks

 Pinterest.com/HarlequinBooks

ReaderService.com

**ROMANCE WHEN
YOU NEED IT**

PGENRE2018

Love Harlequin romance?

DISCOVER.

Be the first to find out about promotions, news and exclusive content!

 Facebook.com/HarlequinBooks

 Twitter.com/HarlequinBooks

 Instagram.com/HarlequinBooks

 Pinterest.com/HarlequinBooks

ReaderService.com

EXPLORE.

Sign up for the Harlequin e-newsletter and download a free book from any series at **TryHarlequin.com.**

CONNECT.

Join our Harlequin community to share your thoughts and connect with other romance readers!
Facebook.com/groups/HarlequinConnection

HARLEQUIN®

**ROMANCE WHEN
YOU NEED IT**

HSOCIAL2018

Earn points on your purchase of new Harlequin books from participating retailers.

Turn your points into **FREE BOOKS** of your choice!

Join for FREE today at **www.HarlequinMyRewards.com.**

Harlequin My Rewards is a free program (no fees) without any commitments or obligations.

MYR18